Billy Bowater

BILLY BOWATER

A Novel

by E. C. Hanes

Rane Coat
PRESS

Distributed by John F. Blair, Publisher
1406 Plaza Drive
Winston-Salem, North Carolina 27103
www.blairpub.com

First printing 2014

Design by Debra Long Hampton

Library of Congress Cataloging-in-Publication Data

Hanes, E. C., 1945-
  Billy Bowater : a novel / by E. C. Hanes.
     pages   cm
  ISBN 978-0-89587-633-1 (alk. paper) — ISBN 978-0-89587-634-8 (ebook) 1. Young
men—Fiction. 2. Legislators—Fiction. 3. North Carolina—Politics and government—
Fiction. 4. Washington (D.C.)—Fiction. 5. Political fiction. 6. Legal stories. I. Title.
  PS3608.A71428B55 2014
  813'.6—dc23
                              2014004468

To Jane, my wife and best friend

You shall have joy, or you shall have power, said God, you shall not have both.

Ralph Waldo Emerson, *Journal*, October 1842

Prologue

Senator Wiley G. Hoots
132 Dirksen Senate Office Bldg.
Washington, D.C. 20510
Jan. 9, 1990

Dear Papa,
    I'm sorry so much time has passed between letters, but I've been awfully busy lately. I'm trying to stay in touch better than I have in the past, but I guess sometimes I just get too engrossed in day-to-day problems.
    As you know better than anyone, I am not one to admit mistakes easily; however I must say that you were right and I was wrong as far as Evvie's choice of a university. I guess I still remember our many fights over where I was to go to college and how angry I was when I ended up at Bob Jones. With age comes wisdom, Papa, and I now see your wisdom. Bob Jones gave me a sense of values that are simply not available in most colleges today and certainly not available at The University of North Carolina in Chapel Hill. I guess I was trying to be a modern

mom, in letting my daughter make her own choices in life, good or bad, but what I allowed is a bad choice, one I can't change now.

Being the daughter of Wiley Grace Hoots was never easy, but for better or worse it has molded me into a woman I hope you can now be proud of. As I get older, and hopefully wiser, I see through eyes that for too long fought the lessons and ideals you wanted for me. Such is the penalty of a rebellious youth.

Harvey and I spent last weekend with Evvie in Chapel Hill. We went to several of her classes and spent time with her and her new boy friend, a young man from somewhere in New Jersey. It was eye opening to say the least, and certainly not the college experience that I had or even imagined for myself. Sitting in her classes and listening to her professors gave both Harvey and me the clear understanding that in college today, at least at UNC, there is little room for a student who has strong Christian beliefs. People who live by a code of conduct modeled on a strong personal faith are made to feel ignorant and out of touch there. Chapel Hill seems to relish its reputation as a world in which there are no standards, no code, no moral basis. Do what you want to do; every point of view is valid; there is no right or wrong, only the moment. Is this truly what we have come to?

Trying to end our trip on a high note, Harvey and I went by the Ackland museum to see the Old Master print show hanging there. It was beautiful, but on the way out, we went through some galleries displaying a contemporary show of the work of young artists from "Generation X", whatever that is. These so-called artists' works only proved, yet again, that taste and culture are no longer at the center of the university experience. I will not try to describe the whole show, if indeed I could summon the strength; however, let me say only that standing in front of a painting whose central image is a man, undoubtedly a derelict, leaning against the crumbling wall of a decaying inner city building while urinating on the head of some other unconscious street person, proved to me and Harvey once and for all that this is not the environment we wanted for our daughter and your granddaughter.

What's more, this painting, and I have only partially described its offenses, was only the most obvious affront to good taste. There were numerous other "works of art" that added to the disgrace, photos of naked young girls embracing under waterfalls, for example.

To add a final insult to this injury, the exhibition was paid for in part by the National Endowment for the Arts. So not only are our state taxes being used to fund such trash but our federal tax dollars are compounding the felony. I know that you realize better than I the many wasteful and disgusting things that the government feels compelled to participate in; so, I hope this example of government-sponsored immorality will give you more ammunition in your fight to elevate the morals of this state and country. It's a crime what some in Washington feel they must do in the name of education and culture! I'm sure this comes as no surprise to you.

Anyway, enough of all this, we miss you and hope that you will get home soon. On a positive note, young William is doing well at Christ School; you would be proud of him.

All my love to Mother,

Betsy

1.

I hate mornings.

I hate gargling a product that looks and probably tastes like lighter fluid. The label says Listerine antiseptic mouthwash kills germs that cause gingivitis, whatever that is, I don't care. I just want my mouth to taste better than my head feels.

I got to Raleigh yesterday, a freezing February afternoon, in order to finalize our arrangements for the press conference announcing Wiley's fourth campaign for the United States senate. This was my first major campaign as chief administrative assistant for Wiley Grace Hoots, the senior senator from North Carolina. I'd worked for Wiley for five years in various positions ever since leaving the eastern North Carolina town of Warren and the covetous woman still using my last name. I wanted and have asked for it back, but as usual Sylvia demurred.

When I was growing up, I was told that having a name like William Walpole Bowater the Third would build character and open doors. I didn't believe it. Not that I wasn't proud of the original and subsequent William Walpole Bowater, because I was; however, living in the shadow of such men and the legacy they had created made life hard if you were young, trying to fit in.

Father was, and still is, the managing partner of Bowater & Bass LLC., a law firm established by his father, the original William Walpole Bowater. As if building on his father's firm wasn't enough of a challenge, father, in his mid-forties, ran for and was elected attorney general of North Carolina, and served in that capacity for eight years. After his second term, he returned to Warren and to Bowater & Bass, which by now was both larger and better connected than when he left. One can only assume that serving as attorney general of North Carolina didn't hurt the reputation of either William Bowater Jr. or his firm.

For my whole life the people of Warren assumed that someday I, William the third, would take father's place at Bowater & Bass. It was even hinted, when I was chosen as a Morehead Scholar, that I would inherit his political mantle as well. Of course no one ever bothered to ask my views on the subject. They just assumed.

Bowater and Bass wasn't a regional power because of its size or the wealth of its corporate client base; there were many firms in the major population centers with more partners and bigger corporate clients. Rather, Bowater was the go-to firm for most of the eastern North Carolina legislators, a group of inordinately powerful men. They represented the smallest populations in the state, but once in, they never lost, or did so rarely. The urban legislators, those from Raleigh, Greensboro, Winston, and Charlotte, rotated through the legislature like new-year's resolution dieters through Weight Watchers, but the eastern legislators ruled for decades, grabbing seniority in both houses and holding on to it like feudal barons.

I was the only scion in my generation since Walter and Mrs. Bass had not spawned successfully and I had no brothers or sisters. After college and law school, I went home, as expected, to follow the legal profession as practiced at Bowater & Bass, which is to say that I became nearly catatonic writing wills, papering real-estate transactions, and representing small businesses with their mundane legal needs. I became a professional sleepwalker. Only when I began to represent our clients' needs before the state and federal legislatures, what was called governmental affairs by the partners, did I become rejuvenated and energized. Because of the firm's friends in the legislature, we were highly sought after by organizations seeking "advice," lobbyists' code for buying access.

Though still an associate at Bowater & Bass, it was my clear ambition to move totally into the governmental side of the firm. I saw myself as a modern-day Paladin, a knight-errant who rode from his tyranny each day in search of adventure and new dragons to slay—no rickety windmills for me. I believed myself to be different from those weak, humble souls who forever labored over library books and precedents. I aimed to cut a swath through the law that established new boundaries and set new precedents.

I would create a new position, something solid but also intimidating. Being a lobbyist didn't suit me. Besides, how could "lobbying" describe what was basically a contact sport? Extorting or Convincing or Compensating, or even Coercing would be more accurate, but by whatever name, I loved the chase, the strategizing, and even the greed.

I discovered that in the greed business there were no rules, only conventions. There were no heroes, at least no white-hat, square-jawed, aw-shucks heroes, but there were inspirations, mentors. Mine was a man whom I met at a conference in Washington. He had lived and worked in the capital for over thirty years, and his firm had, at one time, been the most respected and feared in the district. At the conference, a young attorney, a recent partner in one of the large K Street firms, was bragging to J.D., my inspiration, about how much money he billed out each month.

He threw out some outrageous number as his hourly rate, then stood back to see the look of admiration on J.D.'s face. J.D.'s expression never changed, and after a suitable amount of time said to the young legal stud, " Son, when you're hired to win a gunfight, you don't charge by the bullet."

That's where I wanted to go, enough of this repetitious hourly grind. While I enjoyed the precision and security in the law, "the rule of law" as the keepers of the profession liked to say, I found the day-to-day practice stifling. I wanted to improvise, to enter new territory plotting new ideas with new personalities, and until I had an unfortunate brush with the ethics committee of the state bar association, I was becoming productive and happy, at least at work.

My personal life was another matter. Survival had become the objective, and I was losing at that. I had met my wife, Sylvia, while in law school in Chapel Hill and we were married the summer after my graduation. My father had warned me about marrying too soon, but as usual I knew better. Sylvia and I had been happy in Chapel Hill.

But I came to realize that while a halcyon, energetic place, Chapel Hill was a community far removed from the realities of the world. Sadly, relationships begun there were almost guaranteed to wither in the suffocating heat of small-town eastern North Carolina unless you were both from there originally.

Sylvia was from Nashville, Tennessee, and a more acquisitive female has not graced the planet since Eve. Her father had made a fortune in the music business and thus spoiled his three daughters beyond the bounds of reality. When we met, Sylvia was a student at St. Ann's college, a woman's college near Raleigh—a two-year school with one year's worth of classes, what students called, a safety.

Sylvia wasn't a student. She was beautiful, had lots of toys, knew her way around the bedroom, and knew how to make a law student who was trying to be sophisticated feel he was, but she wasn't a student. Making men feel special was a talent that pretty young debutantes in Nashville learned early on. It was how she got daddy to buy her a brand-new sixty-thousand-dollar Mercedes convertible. But looks, Southern charm, and bedroom skills don't carry much water when the talk runs out. Sylvia wasn't dumb, but it became clear under the spotlight of daily life that a complex thought was as lost in her head as a hard-shell Baptist in a liquor store.

I began putting in long hours at Bowater & Bass to avoid going home to Ms. American Express Card and the carping that was worsened by the month. My long hours at work eventually shifted to the country club, long hours of scotch and gin rummy. I began to develop friendships with men who were clearly not helpful to my future, men like Johnny Walker and William Grant.

If you are coming to the conclusion that I was beginning to deteriorate to the point of embarrassment to my father and family, then you are correct. And if you are further coming to the conclusion that a change was in order, then you are correct again. I don't remember exactly when he did it, but at some point father called his lifelong friend, Wiley Grace Hoots, and arranged for his son, the "scion," to become one of the senator's legislative aides.

While this was presented to me as an opportunity to expand my knowledge of governmental law, specifically as practiced in our nation's capital, it was really an attempt to remove a potential embarrassment from the firm and possibly the family. You can't really blame father. After all, he had spent his life building the family name and was in no mood to see William the third raze it. I knew he was right. I also knew that my life with Sylvia was over. Probably a lot of that was my fault. You can't hold someone else up if you feel down. It was time for me to move on.

~

Spitting out my Listerine, I heard a sudden hacking cough from the tight lump in the middle of my king-size bed.

"Hey, you awake?" I said.

"No, I'm coughing in my sleep."

Lucy Sue Tribble twisted under a pile of lime-green blankets and polyester sheets. She was a real picture . . . scruffy black hair, puffy eyes, and the temperament of a snake with PMS.

"Lucy, I've got to go pretty soon. You need anything?"

"I need breakfast. Quiet. A bath. I need—. Why the fuck are you doing that again?"

"Doing what?"

"Looking at me through your fist like it was some kind of damn telescope."

"Judge Parker always said that you could see the world better, or focus on it better, something like that, if you could cut out all the extraneous garbage. So, I've got you, just you, square in my sights. You have my full attention."

"I don't want your full attention. I want you to go away!"

Lucy was always saying things like that, but she didn't mean it. This was about the tenth time in the last few months we had slept together, if you call two hours of rest sleeping. But here's the thing, by six o'clock tonight I'll be a basket case while Lucy will be ready to party. I'll never understand where she gets the energy. I know for a fact she doesn't work out, not even those plotties or whatever. At 120 pounds, she's a featherweight punching up four classes to middleweight. Lucy loves sex the way a Carmalite nun loves praying.

"You know you want me to stay all morning and whisper sweet nothings in your ear."

"Sweet nothing is about what you're worth," she said, pushing her head up out of the blankets and squinting at me through the slits she was using for eyes.

"Billy, listen to me. I don't want you to whisper sweet anythings to me. I want you to get the fuck out of here. I want quiet. I want. . . . " She opened her eyes wide.

"By the way, you look like shit. Standing there with that tiny Hiltonian towel barely wrapped around your ever-expanding middle, you look like a modern Edward Teach."

"Who's Edward Teach?"

"Jesus, why do I associate with such dullards? Blackbeard, you Carolina fool."

"Ah ha! And you have seen Blackbeard?"

Lucy lay back in the bed and mumbled, "What the fuck am I doing here?"

I laughed and turned back into the bathroom for my deodorant.

"I'll bet," I yelled, "That the good Baptists of Wake Forest would be sorely ashamed that one of their honor grads used such coarse, vile language."

"Fuck the Baptists," she mumbled, "fuck the good, for that matter."

Lucy Sue Tribble was unique. She was the best political reporter in the state and had worked for the Raleigh *News & Observer* for a dozen years, including summers during college. She may not have been the daintiest of flowers, but she damn sure was the sharpest thistle in the garden. Between those multi-pierced little ears was a brain that could remember every quote she had ever penned to steno pad. She was at her desk writing articles while the other reporters were still looking up words and tracking down suitable quotes.

She hated jewelry, except for her loop earrings and the BB-sized silver stud that peered out of her more than generous navel. She thought of food as a necessity rather than an anticipated pleasure and she dressed like she had just got waked up by an earthquake. Blousy shirts, jeans, and jogging shoes were her workday wardrobe.

She could dress up when the occasion called for it, though. Last year I picked her up for the White House correspondents' dinner in D.C. and couldn't believe the transformation—rich blue silk evening dress, high heels, and a total cosmetic makeover. I must have looked shocked because the minute I opened my mouth to compliment her, she pounced.

"Not a word, nimrod, or you get nothing tonight."

"I wouldn't dare," I replied, "But please, the startled look is one of admiration and awe. You look beautiful. And my, grandma, what big, uhm, what large—do you have a preferred plural?"

"Well, tits is out. How about mammary glands?"

"Too scientific. How about melons?"

She looked at me sideways.

"Breasts. What lovely breasts you have, grandma." It was a great evening.

One of the many benefits of being the chief AA for Senator Hoots was that I got to enjoy the perks offered to him but rarely accepted. He hated to go out, at least out when others more important to the press than he were there. He could tolerate it if he was the featured attraction; however, at an event like the correspondents' dinner he would be small potatoes.

I loved the show. Anybody who was anybody in Washington, New York, or Hollywood was there. Not that I rated a second look, but one never knew when an important contact would be made or an opportunity present itself. One thing for sure, if you weren't there, nothing could happen.

Lucy was in heaven. After all, it was a party for journalists and Lucy was a natural. She knew every newspaper represented and damn near every major writer for each. She was like a kid coming to Disney World for the first time. Not quite the same as today's event in Raleigh.

Were wishes reality, I would spend the entire morning with Lucy engaged in whatever struck our fancy. A plausible wish since both of our fancies ran to the same conclusions. But it was not to be. I had to get downstairs to prep the staff on this afternoon's press conference. Against my better judgment, I had designated a seat for Lucy on the front row, while praying to the press-conference-gods that she wouldn't start with the gotcha zingers for which she was so famous. All we wanted to do today was to announce Wiley's candidacy, answer a few softball questions, and feed the mob. Think, sermon-on-the-mount lite, featuring soft drinks, cookies, and a little fruit and cheese. We'd leave the fishes-and-loaves trick to our fellow North Carolinian, Billy Graham.

More than the mouth on Lucy, I was nervous about Wiley deciding this really was a sermon-on-the-mount moment and launching into a made-for-TV rant against liberals, the media, and any other group caught in the cross hairs of his morality scope.

Lucy was rummaging around in her purse for a cigarette, so I flipped my pack of camels onto the bed along with my Dale Earnhardt lighter.

"Lucy, please no questions about Castro, Russia, U. N. funding, or abortion. None of that shit, okay?"

Lucy flipped open the lighter and lit her cigarette, squinting at me through her smoke. It wasn't a matter of whether some withering, snide comment was coming, just how profane it would be.

"*That* shit. Well, it does seem appropriate that you would define four of the planks of the Republican party as that shit. However, I'm not sure what we are supposed to ask Herr Hauptmann Hoots if you are exempting the entire party platform."

"Come on. You know what I mean. I don't want you to ask questions just to start a fight."

Lucy smiled. She knew perfectly well what I was talking about. Even with her overly developed crust of cynicism, Lucy Sue was fair. She didn't mind people having different opinions, in fact she enjoyed the debate; however, when she thought a person was mouthing homilies and pompous pronouncements for the sake of a vote, she could be brutal in taking them down.

One evening we were having dinner at a restaurant in Raleigh and the mayor was on television talking about school busing and how he was concerned about the little children being on the bus for so long each day and how neighborhood schools would solve that problem. Lucy had taken about all of his hypocrisy she could. She leaned back in her chair and threw her napkin at the television.

"Time, time out! Fifteen yards . . . unnecessary bullshit!" she yelled, adding a referee-like whistle and a thumb thrust to the side, approximating an out-at-home call. Everybody in the place stopped mid-bite and looked at our table.

"Mr. Mayor," she told the television, "that is not what you told the Republican party executive committee last week. I believe you said something about the dangers of mixing the races, you lying bastard." A waiter picked up the napkin and handed it back to Lucy.

"Ma'am," he said smiling, "I believe you dropped this, and by the way, a thumb to the side is a baseball signal, plus they don't throw flags in baseball."

Lucy smiled and said, "Whatever. One of those ball games." She figured justifiable rage allowed her to mix sports metaphors in calling infractions of the bullshit rule.

~~~

I finished tying my tie and looked around the room for my suit jacket. Thank God it was hanging on the back of the desk chair and not crumpled on the floor. I couldn't be sure since it was after midnight when we got to the room and my compass was out of kilter.

"Okay, so we're straight. You get the first question, but not a zinger. I'm not saying you can't ask tough questions but you know what I mean. Don't embarrass me . . . please."

She rolled to her left and planted her face in the foam pillows. "Ummmkay. I wann sa nuthinnn sitty."

"I interpret that as, okay, I won't say anything shitty. Right?"

She sat back up. "Yes, that is correct, mein Fuhrer!"

"Okay, I'm off. You can call room service. But wait five minutes. And don't sign your name. Just put Bowater on the ticket."

"You ashamed of me, Billy?"

"No, just cautious. I don't want some enterprising young thing from the Raleigh or Charlotte paper to get a whiff of a tryst between William Bowater, AA to Senator Hoots, and Lucy Sue Tribble of the *News & Observer.*"

"Don't worry, most of the eager beavers on those papers think a tryst is something you tie the top of a garbage bag with. Anyway, I'm not going to be here much longer. I gotta run by the office and file my stuff for the metro and state guys."

I nodded, then leaned down and gave her a quick kiss on the mouth. "I'll be in touch."

Lucy took a long drag on her cigarette and said, "Hey, John, you leave my money on the dresser?"

I turned back toward her expecting a sly smile. But Lucy had a cold, hurt expression.

"What?" I said, cuing boyish confusion.

"You heard me."

"Yes, but I don't understand you."

"I mean, Mr. Smoothie, that if you are going to treat me like a whore, then at least pay me like a whore."

There are always moments in a man's life of dealing with the opposite sex where you know you've fucked up big-time. You also know that it's better and safer to pretend innocence than to argue. This was such a time.

I took my coat off my shoulder and went back to the bed and sat down next to her. She looked at me through cold dead eyes. I felt the hurt they spoke to, so I kept my mouth shut until I had properly thought out what I wanted to say.

"Guilty. I was thinking about the guys downstairs, myself, and you, in that order. The order was exactly backwards, and I apologize. The fact is I would rather spend the day with you than almost anything I can think of. I love being with you and I don't say that often enough. I'll do better. Fact is, too, I'm nervous about this upcoming campaign. I've never been the lead dog on the sled. I've always been at the back staring at the assholes, never in front as the lead asshole. I don't want to fuck up. Wiley Hoots does not abide fuck-ups, and running a U.S. Senate race offers lots of opportunities for 'em."

Lucy's expression slowly unfroze and began to approach room temperature. Her lips were still taut and straight, but her eyes had lost their frigid pain. They were mellowing a tad.

"You know," I said, "I'm a lot better at being an AA for Wiley than I was being a lawyer writing wills and divorce papers in Warren. I like Washington, Lucy. I like and understand the people. I watch Wiley's back when the knives are out and hand him one when backs are turned. I know who Wiley needs and who needs Wiley, but I don't delude myself into thinking that I'm the one the people elected.

"Wiley has me around to look after him, and when he thinks I can't do that, I'm toast. He doesn't give a shit what I think about the big issues of the day. He doesn't give a shit what most people think about the big issues. He knows what he thinks and believes. He marches to the beat of a different drummer: a gun in every house, family values,

Christian, white, right-foot-only, bang the drum slowly, drummer. Shit, I don't have his zealotry. I'm packed a lot lighter, Lucy. I'm basically along for the scenery, good times, and resume credits." Lucy finally licked her lips and put on a little smile, eyes first.

"Bullshit. You love it, and you're good at it. Don't give me that humble, head-bowed crap. You're Wiley's AA because you're smart and alert, and you'll put up with his bullshit positions in order to stay in the light. You love the lights, the brighter the better! You're as addicted to the power trip as he is, only you acknowledge it when pressed. He continues to mumble that God has sent him on a mission, but he doesn't fool me, and you can't, either." She put her hand on my cheek and leaned in for a real kiss this time. I hope I didn't disappoint.

I also realized that I didn't want to take this woman for granted. As tough as she was, as cynical and frayed around the edges, she was great fun . . . and smart. She also was right about me. I did love it. I loved the borrowed power—the intrigue. I loved negotiating on issues that would affect the world, not just North Carolina but the world, that large orb sitting on the table in my father's study. I loved the possibility of being different, a William Walpole Bowater forged from alloys not yet contemplated in Warren. I loved everything except the occasional sense of guilt that would close my throat and dry up my spit when conceding points I knew I shouldn't. I told myself that every worthwhile lawyer in Washington and even in North Carolina felt the same way. And I gave this guilt a life-preserver name—compromise—and wore it without reservation.

"I have never," I said, "in my wildest dreams, imagined that I could fool Lucy Sue Tribble. I just hope she knows how much I care for her." I stopped before I said something I wouldn't live up to.

"I gotta go, but thank you dearly, Lucy. I'll see you at the press conference." I kissed her again.

She slapped me on my butt as I stood up. "Okay, Mr. Bowater, get off my bed. Go do your thing. Keep the balloons full of hot air and the plates piled high with steaming BS. The show must go on."

I made an exaggerated gesture of hitching up my pants. When I got to the door, I looked back and smiled. Lucy dropped the sheet from her chest, leaned back in the bed, and pulled the strong Turkish blend into her lungs while waving like the Queen Mother passing in parade.

2.

A lot of people don't like press conferences, but I love 'em. Watching all the camera jockeys and TV techies flying around the room is like watching the fiddler crabs at Pawley's Island scampering about the mud flats looking for a hole. Once they get set up, they feel safe, even superior, to the herd of reporters wandering about in their world.

Everything seemed to be in order, except for the oversized dancing elephant banner hanging behind the podium. It looked like one of those freak-show signs at the county fair—"See Grizzo, half-man half-bear!" I thought we ought to look like a serious enterprise, not some carnival sideshow, but the TV guys said it was a good backdrop for the Senator, so I quit trying to have it taken down. Politics and political functions were so tacky these days no one would notice or care.

I was starting to feel halfway decent about the press conference when I saw Renn Foster, Wiley's finance chairman. If ever an individual could deflate a key moment, it was him.

"Hey, Renn. When did you get in?"

" 'Bout an hour ago. You seen Wiley?"

"Yeah, he's in a meeting room down the hall talking to some guys from tobacco. I thought you were going to meet us at the headquarters."

"Yeah, well, I thought I'd come early. I like these shindigs."

"Uh-huh. But listen, this isn't a fundraising event. I know that Wiley is on your case to fill the coffers, but this isn't the place, okay?"

"Sure, but hey, this isn't my first roundup, Billy."

"It's 'rodeo,' Renn. This isn't your first rodeo."

He rolled his eyes. "Right, but hey, good to see you, ol' buddy."

He stuck out his hand, no doubt excited by the prospect of crushing my every knuckle. Renn is one of those ex-jocks who believes that every handshake is a test of his manhood, so he's not happy unless he gets a bent knee and an audible groan. I grabbed his hand and then quickly let go before suffering any damage.

Mr. Foster is what happens to small-time college football players who can't take their lives out of instant replay. He married a Southern American princess whose daddy owned a car dealership in Wilson, North Carolina. When daddy went to the great showroom in the sky, Renn took over the dealership, and I'm sure starts every day with a mandatory employee prayer circle. No doubt every sale gets the closer a pat on the butt and a manly attaboy.

"Love to talk with you some more, Renn, but I need to brief Wiley on this afternoon's schedule. I'll see you after the show, okay?"

"You bet!" Renn said, adding, "Good luck and God's blessings be with us."

I mumbled something in reply, but don't remember what. It was probably somewhat less than charitable.

⌒

Wiley appeared in the doorway of the conference room fresh from his meeting with the half-dozen lawyers representing the tobacco companies. It usually took that many to carry the bags of money they periodically lavished on senior legislators, and Wiley was one of their favorites. To hear him tell it, tobacco was the next best thing to vitamin C in enhancing the lives of Americans.

Like Wiley, I grew up in tobacco country and even as a children we knew that pulling smoke into your lungs was not the surest path to good health and a ripe old age. But then tobacco was the crop that kept food on the table for most of eastern North Carolina and we couldn't give it up any more than Kentucky could give up bourbon and alcoholics. Besides, tobacco was one of the few subjects on which the senator and I agreed. It says on the pack that smoking can be hazardous to your health, and even if it didn't, you'd have to be dumber than a brick to not realize it.

Wiley looked around the door frame and into the conference room. "Everybody here that we need? My guys from WRUL here?"

"Yes, sir. In fact, Mr. Fletcher Johnson is here in person. He said he would speak with you after the press conference." Wiley had worked as an editorial writer at WRUL for a number of years in his younger days. Fletcher Johnson was the owner of the station and a voice for arch conservatives in the state.

"You know, William, I think I loved working at that station more than at any job I've ever had. Many a day I wondered why the heck I swapped that job for one in Washington playing nursemaid to a bunch of leftist apparatchiks."

"Yes, sir. Well, I'm sure that everybody in North Carolina is glad you did."

I'm good at ass-kissing, and nothing primes a politician going into a press conference more than a big wet smooch on the butt. Wiley smiled his aw-shucks smile and waved to Fletcher Johnson.

"Oh, yeah, you should also know that Daniel Frank from the N&O is coming. His political reporter, Lucy Sue Tribble, will be sitting on the front row. I promised her the first question, being a fellow Wake Forest grad and all." I figured I might as well prepare him since I knew he didn't care for Lucy Sue.

"Umhuh. Well, William, she might be a Wake grad but she sure has strayed from the Baptist way. I hope you told her to keep her sarcasm in check."

"Yes sir, I did. I'm sure it will be fine."

"Okay, let's roll." Wiley said, then did a double-take as he turned away. He leaned back in and said, " Glad you got the old good-luck tie on, William."

"Yes, sir. Wouldn't be without it." Actually, I would love to be without it, but ever since mother gave it to me, I've had to wear this affront to good taste to every public event. She had attended one of my first press conferences with Wiley, and gave it to me while I was talking to the senator. I remember the occasion all too vividly.

"William, I was in this adorable shop in Raleigh and saw this precious tie and just knew it would bring you and the senator good luck. See, it has elephants marching to victory across the front. Isn't it wonderful?"

I believe I made an adequate response, something about good luck charms and fates being with us, but it would have been obvious to anyone who knew me that there was no chance of my wearing such a stupendously ugly tie while I was living and not under the influence of copious quantities of alcohol. The problem arose because Wiley, while smiling broadly at mother, couldn't wait to compliment her and her precious purchase.

"Cornelia, this tie will be William's and my good luck charm from now on, right, William?"

I nodded.

"In fact, William, I want you to wear our tie to every press conference and on every election night." So there I was…doomed for political eternity to look like John Merrick Bowater, the Republican Elephant Man.

~~~

I got a high sign from Ann Murphy, Wiley's press coordinator, and maneuvered the senator toward the lectern.

"Senator, I think they're ready to start."

We walked up and I tapped on the microphones.

"Good afternoon, ladies and gentlemen. My name is William

Bowater the Third and I'm Senator Hoots's chief administrative assistant. Welcome to all! We appreciate you being here. I know you all were expecting Mr. Hoover Leggett, Senator Hoots's campaign manager, to do the introductions today, and I'm sorry that Mr. Leggett couldn't be here. I regret to say that Mr. Leggett is attending the funeral of his mother-in-law, Mrs. Florence Weeks. I'm sure I'm safe in saying that all our prayers are with Mr. Leggett and his wife Deloris on this very sad occasion. Perhaps a moment of silence." I bowed my head and gave it my best graveside sigh. After a sufficient moment of silence to honor the departed Mrs. Weeks, whom no one in the room except for Wiley had ever met, I began again.

"I have, over the past few years, had the good fortune of working with many of you, and to those whom I haven't had the pleasure of meeting, I look forward to doing so in the near future. The future is what we're here to talk about today—our future, yours and mine, the people of this state, and the people of this country. We're here today to officially announce the candidacy, for the fourth time, of Senator Wiley Grace Hoots." Okay, shills, start clapping.

~⌐

I glanced down at a smirking Lucy Sue who was giving me her most delicate non-clap clap, then looked away so as not to laugh or lose my train of thought. As she had so astutely observed in our hotel room, I loved these microphone moments. I loved practicing on a live audience my repertoire of sincere and contemplative expressions. Speeches to hotel-room mirrors were self-flagellation compared to the ecstasy of a live audience.

I looked at my watch. Time to move on. I said that Wiley had been so busy on senate business that he hadn't had the time to come to Raleigh to file until just this week—a lie. We were waiting to see what Governor James, Wiley's opponent, was going to do about his announcement.

"As often happens during an election year, totally unsubstantiated rumors start circulating in the media and are then passed on to the public. To have assumed that Senator Hoots was considering retirement because he didn't file until the last week of the period is, quite simply, absurd. The fact is, because of the senator's prominent position on so many critical committees, he just hasn't had the time to get back down here to Raleigh to file."

I was on a roll. The lies were flowing like fresh honey onto warm biscuits. I thought my look of sarcastic irony was particularly good this afternoon. Too bad I'd have to turn the microphone over to Wiley.

"Now I know that most of the speculation has come from outside the state, from papers like the *New York Times*, liberal elites, hoping that he wouldn't run. As a result, some of you, our long-time friends, may have had a few questions. And that's why Senator Hoots is here today, to answer your questions. So without further ado, I'm proud to present the most dedicated, beloved public servant in North Carolina, Senator Wiley Grace Hoots!"

Wiley stepped up to the podium waving his hand up and down like a schoolchild. He loved this stuff. He was glowing, as Mark Twain once said, with "the confidence of a Christian holding four aces."

"Good morning, my friends. It's always a great pleasure to get back to Raleigh; to see family and friends; to be among real Americans. As to the rumors that Wiley Hoots is packing it in, calling it a day, nonsense! Nobody is going to run Wiley Hoots out of Washington. Of course, I would be lying to you if I said that I hadn't thought, on more than a few occasions, about coming home to the peace and quiet of North Carolina. It's tough waking up every morning knowing that you have to march up to the Hill to fight raving liberals and big-government loonies."

Classic Wiley. Start off with a lot of soapy "us" and "ours," and then move fast to a "damn-the-federal-gov'mint" line.

"Now I would love to come in here and tell the people of this great state that things are fine in America, that honesty and decency are alive and well in the land, but that would be a lie. As someone once said, 'There is something foul in Denmark.' And folks, there's also something foul in America. The liberals are trying harder than ever to take away your rights to control your own lives; secular humanists are untiring in their efforts to keep prayer out of our schools, prayer, by the way, that sustained the founders of this great land during its many times of trouble early on; and pro-abortionists and homosexuals are gaining ground even as we speak.

"My friends, a country that forgets God is committing suicide. So, I intend to stay in Washington and fight until there isn't a breath left in me, though I'm sure the Democrats hope that's soon.

"Well, I said that I wasn't going to give a speech, so how 'bout some questions?"

Wiley looked around the room.

"Ms. Tribble. What does the *Raleigh News & Observer* have on its mind?"

Lucy stood up and smiled. "Senator, I'd like your perspective on your recent attacks on the Supreme Court and its continued support of the constitutionality of *Roe v. Wade*. What . . ."

Wiley cut her off. "I haven't attacked anybody or anything. I don't know what you could be referring to."

"Senator, I'm referring to your speech of last week where you implied that you might join with a group from the FFA in challenging *Roe v. Wade*. Are you going to assist them in mounting another legal challenge to the law?"

Wiley was clearly annoyed, and glanced at me to make sure I saw it.

"Ms. Tribble," Wiley said looking back at Lucy, "I did not say that I would lend my name to a specific legal action by my friends at the Families for America; however, I implied that were I not a U.S. Senator, I might very well."

Wiley answered a few more questions, but it was clear that he didn't want to engage in the usual kind of banter that these press conferences encouraged. Lucy had soured him on going much farther today.

"Listen, folks, I don't want to argue with you people in the media. I understand how it works. You got the pens. You control the typewriters, the presses, the cameras and the broadcast towers. Don't forget that before I served in the senate, I was with WRUL, which I am delighted to see is represented here by Mr. Fletcher Johnson, my old boss or rather my past boss. Age certainly doesn't apply to Mr. Johnson," and he gave a nod to Mr. Johnson, who smiled and waved, then gave a thumbs up.

"I understand the game that some of you folks want to play, but I don't choose to play that game right now. I'm really a right simple sort of man who takes his lead from the average taxpayers in this state, not the media and certainly not from the nabobs in academia."

Nice deflect, "average taxpayer," indeed. Wiley isn't interested in the average taxpayer. Wiley's interested in the average voter. Votes get you back to Washington.

I once worked for a state senator from Warren, a friend of the family, who said to me, "William, all voters are taxpayers, but not all taxpayers are voters. You gotta know who pulls the lever." Wiley understands this truism better than anybody I've ever known. Wiley plays to the voters, to *his* voters, to the people who can be counted on to show up on election day, not the ones who whine and write nasty letters to the newspapers.

Often some political pollster proclaims that Wiley's approval rating among North Carolinians has dropped to such and such a level, well below fifty percent. Wiley always replies, "Gentlemen, the only poll that counts is the one taken at the polling places on election day." For Senator Hoots, the most reliable group of voters in North Carolina is rural, married, church-going, and white. It doesn't matter if they're registered Democrat or Republican, they're socially conservative. You could pour a cup of first-generation urbanite into the mix as well. Folks who live in Winston-Salem, Raleigh, or Charlotte but still carry political genes from towns like Williamston, Warren, or Jefferson. The fears and suspicions of past generations are still too thoroughly embedded in their small-town souls to wash out in the heavy-load cycle of progressive "New South" rhetoric.

Then, of course, there are the highly educated professionals in

North Carolina, people who are uncomfortable with some of Wiley's positions on various social issues, but who, idealism aside, will vote for Satan if he promises to keep their taxes down.

Wiley may be the shrewdest politician I've ever known—sophisticated enough to speak to the money but plain enough to relate to the average voter. Yet behind his façade of humility, is a pool of anger a mile deep. Even as a young man, Wiley had been someone who had to "show 'em." He never could say exactly who " 'em" was, but he knew they were out there.

He could see and hear " 'em" whispering, smirking and laughing at him—some hick thinking that he was good enough to come into their world. Getting even with " 'em" for their careless laughter was a lifelong mission for Wiley. And as he got older, " 'em" grew to include not just urban North Carolinians, but the whole damn country.

Some folks accused him of being mean, but of course he didn't see himself that way—quite the contrary. Wiley figured he was simply doing his Christian duty to help lead the fallen back to the light. America to Wiley Hoots was fundamentally an extension of eastern North Carolina and the values that had nurtured and suckled its people for so long. For him these core principles constituted a foundation for the resurrection of the American spirit.

I had always figured that Wiley's posturing was simply a ploy to stay in Washington, but the longer I worked for him the more I came to understand that he really did believe he was on a restorative mission for God. Sometimes I hoped that my initial instinct was right, because a true believer is far more dangerous than a glib phony, and a true believer, like Wiley, tired of being laughed at and carrying a bellyful of rage is the most dangerous creature of all.

I curled a fist into my Judge Parker tube and looked out over the crowd. Most of the troublemakers were gone. Daniel Frank had left halfway through the event. I trained my gaze on Lucy, but if she saw me, she wasn't going to give me the satisfaction of acknowledging it. After another five minutes and a few more soft-ball questions lobbed by friends, Wiley thanked everyone for coming, then looked over at me and nodded. I stepped forward.

"Ladies and gentlemen, I know we're all excited and relieved to know that Senator Hoots will continue on in Washington the fight he began eighteen years ago. We thank you, Senator Hoots!"

The shills applauded and cheered while the more moderate media types politely clapped a few times, then closed their notebooks and sheathed their pens.

3.

With Wiley's departure, the room and everyone in it exhaled and slowly returned to normal. Spotlights were turned off, microphone cables coiled and stored, and the everyday chatter of retreating technicians filled the room and exit halls. Eventually the only noise was the muffled sound of conversations between the small group of reporters who had stayed behind to scavenge cookies and soft drinks. Their small talk sounded like an excuse to keep from going back to their offices and real work.

I looked around to see if there was anyone left worth speaking to when I noticed the stunning new reporter from WRUL preparing to leave. As I recalled from my earlier conversation with Ann Murphy, our media guru, the woman had only been with the station a few months. I walked over to where she was packing her bag.

"Excuse me, Ms . . . ?"

"Scott. Jane Scott."

"May I call you Jane?"

"Sure."

"Jane, I'm William Bowater, Senator Hoots' AA. Since this is your first time covering one of the senator's press conferences, I thought that perhaps I could . . ." I felt a tap on my shoulder.

"Excuse me," I said, turning around. There, with a snide smile, stood Robert Gaylord Fitzpatrick, my roommate at Chapel Hill. Finding it difficult to stay indignant, I said under my breath, "You asshole," then remembering the reporter, turned back to see if there was anything to salvage.

"Jane, I'm sorry that this rude gentleman has interrupted our conversation. You must forgive him. You see, he's from a very backward part of the state and doesn't know better. Perhaps we can continue our conversation later . . . over drinks?"

She smiled. "Thanks, Mr. Bowater, but I really need to get back to the station. Maybe some other time," she said and hustled away. Except for the fact that she'd practically left skid marks, "some other time" had possibilities.

Robert shook his head.

"Sorry, sport. Guess you were just coming to the good part? Maybe you could . . ."

"Shut the hell up."

Robert smiled and put out his hand.

"It's been too long, Robert." I said, holding his hand. "Good to see you."

"You're right, it has been too long. None of your old school buddies have heard a word from you in forever. In fact, given the senator's extensive list of enemies, I assumed that you'd probably been taken hostage by a cell of eco-terrorists or a coven of homosexual abortionists."

I nodded, while pursing my lips. "Actually, a gang of crazed Sierra Club leaf wranglers did make a move on our office a few weeks ago, but we beat them back with the help of some NRA lobbyists down the hall. It was messy, though—there's still blood, bark, and roots all over the floor." Robert laughed and shook his head.

It was good to see a friend, especially one as tried and true as Robert. Hard to imagine that the apprehensive young man I first encountered almost seventeen years ago in front of Craige Hall and the distinguished barrister who stood before me now were the same person. His smile was whiter and straighter, no doubt the result of dental work costing more than the average North Carolina house. Robert's jeans and tee shirt had morphed into a subtle pin-striped suit hand stitched by some Italian clothier who charged by the inch. His burgundy suspenders were embroidered from top to bottom with fly rods and trout flies.

Before he could say anything, I put a finger to my mouth. Nothing must be said until I had finished my inspection. He just smiled and adjusted, with perfectly manicured fingers, his round tortoise-shell glasses, no doubt made or licensed by the same Italian firm that made the suit. If there is a better example of the ugly duckling becoming the beautiful swan, I don't know it.

"So, Robert, what brings the newest full partner of Jinthum and Fandors to our little press conference? Finally coming to your senses and switching parties?"

"No, actually I was here at the hotel to address the N.C. Hog Farmers Association. I saw on the hotel schedule board that the Wiley and Billy show was in town, so when I finished with my clients, the swine merchants, I thought I'd drop by on the off chance that I could catch the dynamic duo before they left town."

"I'm honored that a man of such import would even consider stopping at the modest workplace of two humble public servants." Robert rolled his eyes and held up his hand.

"Please, spare me the public-servant speech, but I'm glad to see that the high-sarcastic wit of William Walpole Bowater has not been dulled by his sojourn in our nation's capital. And by the way, 'humble' has never been a modifier applied to you or to Senator Hoots."

I couldn't help smiling. I had been far too careless in corresponding with Robert. He was a good friend and we had something that was rare and hard to find these days . . . time in grade. I've never had an overabundance of friends—acquaintances, yes, but not friends. Friends take time; they can't be cooked on broil. Friends need slow baking and time to cool.

Robert had seen me in my good times and bad times. He saw me cruel and saw me kind. He saw me happy and saw me sad.

College had been a time of discovery for us. For me, it was the first time that I could be William the Third without reference to the first or second. Most of my classmates at Chapel Hill had no clue who the Bowaters were, and if they knew they didn't much give a damn. Robert and I pledged the same fraternity, dated from the same sororities, and had the same major. Hell, he knew me better than my own father.

My memories of Father while growing up were of a man constantly on the go. If not working at the firm, he was in Raleigh dealing with the state's legal matters. In fact, for most of the eight years he was attorney general, he spent more time in Raleigh than in Warren. He and mother bought a house in downtown Raleigh so he wouldn't have to commute so much.

By the time father was elected attorney general, I was already away at boarding school in Virginia. The Bowaters had attended Woodberry Forest School since the nineteenth century, and they weren't about to break that tradition with me.

My earliest years were spent in a comfortable, but not grand, house in the best section of Warren. I was cared for by a black nanny, Sophie Neal. Mother would, of course, dart in and out of baby duties as it suited her, but Sophie did most of the heavy lifting. She's quite old now but still alive, and if a person can be compared to an object, Sophie is my security blanket.

When I was nine or ten, we moved into my grandfather's house—my mother's father. My mother, Cornelia Spruill, was from one of the wealthiest families in eastern North Carolina. The Spruills owned thousands of acres of prime farmland that produced tons of tobacco, corn, soybeans, and cotton. They had the biggest cotton gin in ten counties, and dozens of tenant farmers paying rent. Grandfather Spruill always told Father that I should be a farmer instead of a lawyer; law was for lazy people and crooks, while farming had been the calling of generations of Southern gentlemen. You can imagine the voiced emotions that reverberated in our house at Christmastime.

When Grandfather Spruill died, mother inherited the house and decided that we should carry on the traditions of the Spruill legacy. Father was not particularly fond of the idea because he didn't want to keep up such a large house, but, as usual, Mother won out. Truthfully, it didn't matter much either way because Father was rarely home. Work was his life, and family, while expected and appreciated, was not the center ring in his tent. We were performers in the side rings, important as supporters of the show and even its future, but not the main attraction. It wasn't that Father didn't love me or Mother, it was just that we needed to assume his love, because he would never say he loved us. I spent my whole young life trying to make him proud, though knowing that even if he was, he would never say it or show it. He simply expected me to succeed.

Expectations are cruel. They're ghosts, without form or substance. They plague your days and haunt your nights, never showing themselves. You occasionally catch glimpses of them in the eyes of relatives, friends, and even curious bystanders, but you never meet them face to face. Sometimes, though, you can hear them whispering things like, "People expect more from you, William" or "A Bowater stands for better than that."

So who in particular was I supposed to be? Where would my grade be recorded when I failed or when I succeeded, and who would decide? Who would let me know that I could finally relax and go on to something that I wanted to do?

I always compared myself to Father and Grandfather based on what others said about them. They were supposed to be my most art-less teachers, but they never saw themselves that way. They felt they were to be my examples, not my buddies. Yet I longed for that pat on the shoulder or glance that said, "way to go."

At some point during my time at Chapel Hill, I can't remember the exact year, I began to imagine what my life's portrait would look like. On my up days, I saw the image of a well-respected, elegant man admired far and wide. On my down days, I saw a pale version of my father. I saw Dorian Gray Bowater, young-looking and untried into old age.

Robert was my fellow traveler. Although from a very different background, one without crushing expectations, he too was trying to imagine who he was to be. We baked in the Chapel Hill oven for seven years, and have cooled for even longer.

⌒

"Listen, Robert, I've got to go back tonight but how about a quick shooter in the bar?"

"Okay, but it's gotta be quick. I've got some work to do tonight for an arbitration tomorrow." I patted him on the shoulder as we walked toward the lobby and the small pub at its far end.

The Elizabethan Room at the Hilton was predictably dark. The wood and fabrics, meant to pass for sixteenth-century English, looked more like early twentieth-century Disney. We picked two stools at the nearest corner of the bar and sat down, elbows propping us up. The waitress, a woman of Titian-like proportions, wandered over and said, "You boys look like bourbon."

I countered, "Scotch, actually, single malt if you've got it."

Robert said, "You were right about me, dear. I'll have Makers Mark on the rocks with a splash of branch."

When the drinks came, I held up my glass, and looking at Robert through the amber liquid, said, "May we always see the darkness through a glass clearly."

He smiled and we clicked glasses, "Whatever that means," he replied.

"It means just what you think it means," I said, swallowing the warm liquid.

Robert thought for a moment. "So, Billy, what's it like in the center ring of the circus?"

"Not bad, in fact, exciting at times. It's stressful, with long hours, but still there're a lot of benies. For example, I have my own parking space in the garage next to the Capitol. Since becoming the senator's AA, I have my own office—probably the size of your coat closet at Jinthum and Fandors. I live in a Georgetown apartment costing more per month than would the whole town of Warren, were it rented out. And—what else? Oh, the big one: franking—I get to mail letters free. Of course you wouldn't know that since I've been so shitty in writing to you."

Robert laughed, "Well, that works both ways. I haven't been too good at sending letters in your direction either."

Another smile-shaded silence descended. Finally Robert said, "Billy, is being the main man for Saint Wiley what you thought it would be?" This sounded more condescending than I liked.

"Saint Wiley? Are we being facetious or just trying to start an argument?"

Robert pursed his lips. "Neither. I'm just asking what it's like to be the lead dog for a man with such a strong agenda. I mean, come on—Wiley has one of the most controversial personalities in Washington. There's nothing he doesn't have a strong opinion on and no issue that he isn't prepared to condone or damn based on his personal agenda. I guess I just have never seen any subject on which you feel that strongly, so I wondered how you got along with him."

I took another sip. Did I just get a compliment or a dig? It sounded more like a dig. "I see. So you don't think there's anything about which I can truly feel passionate?"

"I didn't say that or I didn't mean to say that. I mean that the things Wiley is famous for, anti-abortion, homophobia, limited civil rights, major defense spending, a gun in every glove compartment, etc., have always seemed to be issues that you and he wouldn't agree on."

"Robert, unless I'm mistaken, the name William W. Bowater didn't appear on the last ballot. I'm not the one the people elected, so what I think is irrelevant. I'm sure you don't agree with everything your firm does or everyone it represents, but that doesn't keep you from cashing its checks.

"I'm the same way. I do a job and that's to keep the senator informed, on time, and focused. If he wants my opinion he'll ask for it, and as of now he hasn't and I haven't expressed it. Truthfully, Wiley doesn't want anybody's opinion, but what he does want is for things to go his way. I try to make that happen. Washington, as you well know, is about power, its acquisition and its maintenance, so I try to make sure that he has the power he wants and needs. I'm his enabler as well as his influence accountant. I manage the balance sheet. Who owes Wiley and who does Wiley owe. What are our assets and what are our liabilities. Who's trying to fuck us and who do we need to fuck. Get the picture?"

Robert twisted his drink between his fingers, then took another sip. "Kind of mercenary."

"No. Mercenary is producing ads that encourage people to sue somebody on the basis that they won't have to pay unless they win. In which case the lawyers will take damn-near forty percent of the settlement or verdict. Mercenary is getting appointed trustee in a bankruptcy so you can bleed the estate while screwing the creditors.

"Shit, half the men in your firm would represent Goebbels if he had enough money, and they'd justify it based on the self-serving myth that everyone deserves a lawyer. I went to law school, Robert. I practiced law at the prestigious firm of Bowater & Bass, and every day I saw our clients pay for favors from the legislature so they could gain some advantage. Christ, I was the one carrying the bag and doling out the money! The only difference is that now I'm the one they're trying to bribe. That's just the way the world works.

"What doesn't work is you affecting some Joan of Arc persona, 'cause that dog won't hunt. We're both swimming in pools of shit, Robert—the only difference is that mine is big enough to have waves."

Robert sat there silently taking in all the venom I was spewing out. He didn't say anything, but I could tell he was disappointed. His smile was gone, replaced by a frown fixed beneath downcast, half-closed eyes. He was staring into his drink, perhaps looking for a higher purpose in his friend or at least wanting him to be unchanged from freshman year.

Whatever he was thinking was obviously upsetting him. But then what was I supposed to do. He was a big boy, or should be. Deep down I probably wanted him to agree with, thus reinforce, the propriety of my expressed cynicism, but apparently I hadn't presented a convincing case. I'd only shot off my mouth. Well, it wasn't the first time and likely won't be the last.

He looked up and cleared his throat. "Billy, do you think that maybe you need a break? I mean, you look tired and you're certainly not the same love-the-law kind of guy you used to be."

I rolled my eyes. "Love-the-law kind of guy? Robert, have you forgotten that this love-the-law guy almost got censured by the state bar for wrongful solicitation? I still can't believe that that group of sanctimonious hypocrites continues to condone what is advertised every day on television, and then slams me for something that was trivial by comparison. Love the law . . . how about fuck the law!

"And by the way, when you're part of the machine that makes the laws, your love-the-law feelings take a big hit. Laws today are simply the fabricated rules that a compromised legislature passes to placate and lubricate its patrons. Or to put it another way, laws are passed to reward the executives of companies like those your firm represents, the graft-loving Atlantic Powers, Citizens Banks, and Continental Petroleums of the world, in exchange for giving away obscene amounts of campaign money and, I believe the term is, 'lifestyle embellishments'?"

This seemed to be the final salvo. Robert nodded his head and finished his drink. "Right, I got it. Fuck the law. Grab all the power you can get. Screw family and home. Right." He pushed his stool back with a loud scrapping sound and stood up.

"Billy, good luck. I hope you find whatever it is you're looking for."

I shook my head. "Robert, stop with the wounded-baby-bird routine. Are you telling me that you're shocked by any of this? That I'm telling you something that you didn't already know? Come on, get real. All I'm guilty of is being a lot less graceful in the telling than you're used to."

Robert turned to face me. "I'm not that naïve, Billy. I know how the world works. Maybe the difference between you and me is that I choose not to accept the really shitty parts. I can't be the conscience for everyone in my firm, but I can follow my own. I don't know—I just do the best I can, but Billy, I gotta admit, you've really been on a trip this time." He put out his hand. I took it and held it, not a Renn hold, but a firm grip. No agenda.

"You look tired, my friend. Something's different here. Try and keep some balance, and write or call me on occasion. Let me know you're still alive. And if you find a big fat corporation that's got its tit in a government ringer and needs some legal help to pull it out, send 'em my way," Robert said. I pushed my stool back and smiled.

"And if one of your cash-laden clients needs a friend on Capitol Hill, send 'em my way. I'm always trying to *help* a constituent."

We dropped hands and Robert turned around, slowly making his way toward the hotel lobby, his new Mercedes, then the serenity of his Raleigh office. I slumped against the bar and watched him go. Just as he left the room, he turned and gave me a wan smile and a half-hearted wave. It was, after the way I had just behaved, all I deserved. I waved back and tried to smile.

I looked down the bar and raised my hand to catch the waitress's eye. When she finally looked up I said, "Miss, another Macallan's, please."

She poured the drink, paying little attention to how much of the expensive liquid went into the glass, smiled at me, then slowly slid-walked the five or six steps that separated us and set the half-full glass down on the bar in front of me.

"Hope it helps, sugar," she said, with that knowing bartender smile.

I nodded and mumbled, "So do I."

I turned it around a few times, then slowly raised the glass to just above eye level. I cocked my head to the side and looked through the glass somewhere between the Macallans and the rim. The entrance to the Elizabethan Room was dark and Robert was gone.

"May we always see the darkness through a glass clearly. Here's to you, Robert. We're still baking so don't give up."

4.

It felt more like July than mid-May. The room was hot and muggy and the air conditioning was on the fritz again. Late-afternoon sun shone through the trees at the north side of capitol square and directly into conference room 459, the last along an interminable green corridor on the fourth floor of the Dirksen Senate Office Building. The stale heat in the room matched the dispositions of the five men slumped around the table.

The architects for the Dirksen Building were no doubt selected based on their success in designing federal hospitals for the criminally insane. Neo-Nazi facades fronted corridors wide enough to accommodate five inmates walking abreast . . . footsteps echoing from marble floors to stucco ceilings and back.

No paintings adorned the walls of the Dirksen Building, no comfortable furniture stood about, and no laughing stream of employees crowded its hallways, just harried, self-important legislative staffers festooned with plastic I.D. tags and sour expressions skulking along the cloistered halls of power.

⌐⌐⌐

I sat at the head of the eight-foot-long, oval conference table covered with empty soda cans, wads of legal-pad paper and three-ring binders. Only one window lit the room, and that was at the far end, just behind my chair.

Next along the table was Willis Horton, one of the two founding partners of Carter & Horton, Wiley's political advisors since 1978. Beside Willis was John Carter, the firm's other founding partner, a man frequently referred to by Washington Democrats as "John the Baptist" because of his client list of Christian Coalition conservatives. Over the past dozen years, he and Willis had been responsible for the successful elections of dozens of right-wing politicians.

At the far end of the table sat Renn Foster, half-asleep, the other half bored and witless. Renn was the only member of the committee out of place in a strategy session. A hard worker when pointed in the right direction, Renn was slow to understand the subtleties of a major campaign. Given a list of contributor names, a dollar goal, and a pat on the butt, he couldn't be stopped, but knocking on doors and making phone calls wasn't the object of today's meeting.

Across the table from Willis and John, sat Hoover Leggett, Wiley's campaign chairman, the final member of the group. Hoover had served six terms in the North Carolina state senate, and was one of those ex-legislators who wore his title for life, even after being beaten by a young black attorney in the '84 election. Hoover took the defeat hard. It meant that he had to return to his law practice full time. It also meant he had to deal with what he assumed were disloyal friends and neighbors. He couldn't stomach being beaten by a black man, hadn't even imagined it before the election night's final tally. Hoover was a child of days gone by, an American Miniver Cheevy.

Starting in the late 1960s, North Carolina developed a reputation, as far as race relations were concerned, as one of the most moderate states in the South. Its educational system is better than in most Southern states and the general attitude of the public is more tolerant. If there is an area of racial conservatism though, it's in the east. Eastern North Carolina is the most rural and the most socially conservative part of the state, and it's from this background that Wiley and Hoover have emerged.

It's my background as well, but only because you have to be born somewhere. My family background, on my father's side, the Bowater side, was different. Why the Bowaters developed a reputation for moderation, I don't know. It just happened. Somewhere back down the line, a Bowater passed down a gene that told him, "The Declaration has it right—all men are created equal," and every Bowater since has lived by that trait.

⌒

The 1990 senate race in North Carolina gave every indication of being one of the most expensive in the state's history. There was no fundraising competition from a presidential or gubernatorial race, and the congressional races were, as usual, small change compared to a senate race.

Being the incumbent, Wiley had a distinct advantage in the fundraising wars, but ex-Governor Randolph James, his likely Democratic opponent, was one of the most effective money raisers in the entire South. He was one of the few politicians who actually seemed to love asking for money. He probably would have denied it, but nobody can be that good at something and hate it. The first financial reports weren't due for a month, but the rumor mill had James at five million dollars already, with Wiley a million behind.

"It's only the middle of May, for Christ's sake, and already the bastard has over five million dollars," Renn whined. "Somebody needs to check his basement for a printing press."

He was obviously annoyed, and hours of haggling over pert charts, market strategies, and media options hadn't helped his humor. He was pouting, irritated at his exclusion from much of the conversation.

"I'll bet Governor James's offices aren't this hot," Renn concluded.

⌇

Wiley had always been able to raise large sums of money outside North Carolina because the RNC had always been able to tout him as a conservative who could win. He was the true believer, the protector of American ideals, but now that he was in a position to take over the foreign relations committee if the Republicans won the senate, loyal Democrats everywhere were rallied to the cause of defeating him. They could no longer dismiss him as a poster child for extremists. Money to defeat Wiley Hoots was flowing into Governor James's coffers like tithes into a Billy Graham crusade.

John Carter stood up, put his hands on his hips, bent backward and said, "Okay, gentlemen, it's hot and we're all tired so let's recap." We would be here for another hour. I couldn't take another hour or another minute of John's lectures on "Politics is a blood sport" or "Now's the time to ring the register." John was a bottomless pit of hackneyed political clichés, but he found it difficult to maintain his equanimity when dealing with Renn Foster, or me, for that matter. He didn't like amateurs and Renn was a true amateur. I, on the other hand, was smart enough to keep John off balance and sarcastic enough to be mildly amusing, so he tolerated me off and on.

John had lived in Washington ever since enrolling at Georgetown. I couldn't remember where he'd originally come from, not that it mattered. He'd absorbed the ways and means of the District as if through his pores. The place was as habitual to him as breathing.

After getting a law degree from the University of Maryland, he set about to make his mark in the hallowed halls of the nation's capital, but not as a lawyer. John wasn't about the law. Law was just his credential. John was about money. He loved money. He dressed like money; he ate like money; he lived like money. Money was his substance and power.

his religion, enacting the rights of power, was a corollary of money. Lots of money, lots of power. Twins joined at the hip.

John turned to Willis, "Willis, why don't . . ." I jumped in before we could get ramped up on Willis's recap.

"John, I think we all know where we are. We're in a fight. We have a strong opponent and we need money. Do we really need to prolong this meeting with restating what we already know?"

His expression spoke volumes. Volume one went something like, "Fuck you, Billy, who the hell do you think you are to question me?" Volume two was more of the same but added an epilogue: "If you're so smart, why don't you tell us what to do?" I smiled my best fake smile and decided to wrap up this harangue.

"Gentlemen, I think we're all on the same track. John, you and Willis have kept us focused and heading toward the goal. Don't you think so, Hoover—and Renn?" I looked around to get a positive reply from Hoover and at least a nod from Renn. Both accommodated me.

"Right. Now don't get me wrong, I'm not trying to pry into your and Willis's bailiwick, I just don't think we need to rehash our positions."

John didn't move or say anything for a satisfactory amount of time to reiterate volume one, then stood up and, looking only at Hoover and Renn, said, " Okay, no rehash, but Billy, I am curious about one thing."

He paused, obviously waiting for me to ask "What?"

So I accommodated him. " What are you curious about, John?"

He looked at me. "What's the story on that fucking commercial I saw yesterday?"

I waited a few beats, looked at Hoover and then back at John. "The fucking commercial . . . aha. Well, John, good question. I'm not sure I recall making a commercial to advertise fucking, but if you're referring to our most recent campaign advertising, then I must have missed something in the message."

John didn't blink. "Yeah, like the point."

"I see. We missed the point. Whose point . . . yours or ours?"

"Wiley's point. The campaign's point. The fucking election's point!" John replied. I glanced over at Hoover to see how he was reacting to this sophomoric exchange.

"Basically, John, we updated the '84 profile piece that you and Willis made. We wanted to highlight Wiley's increased seniority, his uncompromising stand on family values, and his growing image as an elder statesman. It's a lot of the same shots from before; however, I'm not sure that I recall any fucking scenes."

John was leaning forward with his chin on his hands. "Maybe that's because you weren't the one getting fucked. Wiley was. And effective? Effective for what? Putting the public to sleep? Like you said, I made the goddamn thing. I know what it was intended to do, and that didn't include raising big money. If you think that weak-ass piece of shit will put bucks in the bank, then Renn was right; we're fucked."

"There's that word again," I said.

Renn looked up. "I didn't say we were fucked."

John looked at him. "You should've." He looked back at me. "I talked to the folks at Compton and they said you and Hoover canceled the piece we'd agreed upon. They said you told them the piece with the partial-birth abortion clips was off limits. Billy, Carter & Horton is campaign consultant here. We call the shots in this campaign. Advertising is, as you said, *our* bailiwick. I thought we were clear on that."

I looked at Hoover. "Senator, am I not correct in my recollection that Wiley asked you to be," I looked back at John and Willis, "the chairman of this campaign? As in 'the one in charge,' and didn't you and I agree that the introductory ad this season should be somewhat more . . . ," I made an exaggerated gesture toward the ceiling, "even-handed and non-controversial? That intentionally antagonizing voters with such graphic shots early on would simply play into the hands of a strong moderate opponent?"

Hoover switched his gaze from me to John Carter. "Well, actually, John, I think I said the other day that showin' them aborted babies was a bit over the top. We can certainly agree or disagree that what we ran is not hard-hitting enough, but I just don't like seeing them babies."

"Well, that's the point, isn't it?" John said, "Nobody likes seeing the babies. That's why they get mad. That's why they rise up out of their Lazy-Boys and shake their fists at the T.V. and scream, 'Enough dead babies! Wiley, you got to stop this sacrilege!' That's when we got 'em.

"Then we can run the profile piece when we have Governor James on the ropes and we're trying to look noble. Right now we need money . . . and lots of it." He turned to his right and looked at Renn, sitting with his hands drooping by his sides and his mouth open. "Renn has a point; we're sucking hind tit in the money department. I'm not saying we would spend all the money right now; in fact, I've reminded everybody why we wouldn't, but we need to have it. We're gonna need lots of it. We gotta have options.

"Which gets us back to the point; we need to start scaring the shit out of people. A truism of politics, gentlemen . . . feel-good platitudes don't bring in money. Fear and anger bring in money." John looked over at Hoover, "I bet you agree with that, Senator."

Hoover ran his fingers through his generous crop of white hair and nodded.

I stared at John Carter with as much eyeball venom as I could muster. "John, I don't want to argue with you about effective scare tactics, that being your specialty, but the truth is that even if we could agree, we don't have the bucks right now. We're trying, believe me. Renn and Wiley and Hoover and I are pulling out all the stops; we're making the calls, but people just don't want to hear it yet. Politics is a fall thing. All they're thinking about now is spring and bunny rabbits and little ducks and goddamn daffodils. We felt the profile piece was a good way to start. It puts a positive foot forward."

John snorted. "We don't have money 'cause we haven't pissed people off. And we ain't likely to by showing them pretty pictures narrated by Mr. Rogers."

Hoover crossed his hands over his stomach and leaned back, giving the impression of having something on his mind.

"Hoover, you're a veteran. You still agree with Billy about our abortion ads?"

Though often swollen with pomposity, Hoover Leggett was a clever and observant politician. When he was sure he had everybody's full attention, he said, "Listen, gentlemen, we're all on the same side here. We can disagree without being disagreeable." He spread his doughy smile around the room like a holiday baker. "John, I agree that an aggressive approach might be more effective as a fundraising tool than our softer approach, but I also think that the ad you envision is too... gross. Those partial-birth pictures will have people running out of their family rooms and into their bathrooms. Perhaps we could piss them off, to use your delicate turn of phrase, John, without making them lose their dinner."

It was enough to get a laugh or smile from everybody there. John held up his hand and said, "Thank you, Senator. It's always good to get a little dose of reality." Everybody looked relieved. John spread his hands out on the table in front of him and paused. "You know, it might be time to borrow a little money in order to place a bet at the show window. People know that Wiley can pull in the bucks, so isn't it logical to believe they'll front us a little money early in the campaign?" It was a rhetorical question, so nobody spoke.

"Hoover, Wiley's been a friend to the banking lobby; surely they have good memories. And surely they understand what a friend like Wiley can mean. Don't you 'spose that the boys down at Citizens Bank can advance a friend a little walk-around money?"

Hoover nodded his head. "I'll call Hugh in the morning."

John took his hands off the table and formed them into a pyramid in front of his mouth. He stared at the far wall and started mumbling into his hands, more to himself than to anyone else in the room. "Wiley is known as a battler; we need a battle to fight. If no dead babies, what? Communists aren't believable. Guns are too narrow. . . ." He continued his ramblings while all the rest of us kept quiet and waited for his conclusion.

"Gentlemen," John said, "Know this: summer is money-raising time, and regardless of what people may or may not be thinking these days, Billy, it's our job to get their minds right. After Labor Day, Wiley will be giving canned speeches, eating cold barbecue, and kissing babies. He ain't gonna have time to make ads or tend to particulars. We need a horse to ride this summer—something that can dominate the papers and make people mad."

"We need to get people's minds into politics and away from the beach. We need the one- and two-hundred-dollar guys; the meat-and-potatoes folks who care about issues they can understand—school prayer, taxes, family values. 'Wiley Hoots, the man from Warren' isn't a punch in the gut, it's a handshake. We need a punch!"

Just then another voice chimed in from the back of the room, "Gentlemen, it shouldn't be too tough to come up with a horse for this race; there're plenty to choose from in Governor James's stable." Wiley had slipped into the room during John's tirade.

"Senator, we didn't hear you come in. We were just laying out a communication strategy for the early part of the campaign," I volunteered.

Wiley nodded. "So I heard, but seems to me like y'all are getting a bit twisted in your underwear. Governor James has made a hundred speeches over the past four years on things like pro-choice, waiting periods for handguns, elimination of prayer in school, government-financed smut, equal rights for homosexuals, quotas for blacks. How long do I have to go on? He's written the menu, just order from it."

John Carter smiled, "Eloquent as usual, Senator, but the problem seems to be money, or more specifically, the current lack of money."

"Well, I'm sure that five such intelligent men can find some small pocket of cash with which to shoot a new ad. Hoover, you ought to be able to call one of those shylocks down at Citizens Bank. Hugh Crutcher has never had a problem asking us for help after one of his egotistical fiascoes. Didn't we call the bank examiners off his case a few years ago?"

Hoover nodded, then added, "Wiley, I mentioned to John just a few minutes ago that I would call Hugh. Billy and I will get in touch with him first thing in the morning."

Wiley smiled then started to leave, but before walking out, he turned back.

"Gentlemen, this is gonna be the toughest race I've ever run. So I'm giving you fair warning, kiss the wives and pack the bags, 'cause you ain't coming home for a long time."

The door snapped shut, and we sat there listening as Wiley's footsteps echoed down the long marble corridor.

John Carter smiled and then laughed out loud. "And which wife would that be, Wiley? I've had four—so far!"

5.

My head hurt and my mouth tasted like the inside of a sweat sock. Why the hell was I climbing four flights of stairs before eight A.M.? I could say that I'd turned over a new leaf and was trying to get back in shape, but then it's pointless to lie to oneself. Truth is I was showing off for Tina Kelso, Senator Davis's new legislative assistant, a runner with long legs, a tight ass, and a gravity-defying bust.

"Hey, Tina, hot enough for you? Yeah, me too, but I like taking the stairs. Keeps me in shape. Damn, here already; doesn't seem like four floors. Okay, see you around." Chest heaving, I staggered into the office, hoping I could get through the door and past Ruth Lee without being seen.

"Good morning, Mr. Bowater. The senator asked for you to come into his office as soon as you arrived."

"Okay, tell him I'll be in as soon as I get organized for the day. Shouldn't take but a few minutes." I made it into my office before I started to wheeze again.

My life in Washington had begun to feel like a never-ending journey along some purgatorial mobius strip that ran from the Dirksen

Building, through downtown, across the bridge into Georgetown and back again. Along the way was a surprisingly ordinary collection of bars, clubs, and eateries. Since I had tried almost all of these, my nightly selection was now governed by finding the establishment with the closest parking place. I did okay last night, but barely.

After checking the calendar for the day, my notes from the staff meeting, and my current to-do list for the senator, I was ready. I slapped my face, pinched my cheeks, and popped an Altoid.

"Ruth Lee, anything I should be aware of. Any problems, calls, sore points I need to anticipate?"

As usual, Ruth Lee replied in her prune-infused voice, "The senator is in a most equitable mood. I'll tell him you are finally here." *Finally* . . . oh how she caressed that word. She seemed to swirl it around, savoring it like a sip of fifty-year-old Napoleon brandy. *Finally here;* I was gratified to give her a moment of joy in her desiccated life.

Wiley was sitting behind his desk reading the *Washington Post.*

"Billy, it never ceases to amaze me how these cowards get away with such nonsense. Listen to this bilious claptrap . . . 'Yesterday afternoon during the meeting of the Senate Foreign Relations Committee, Senator Hoots, the ranking minority member, again displayed his famous penchant for the overly dramatic. When the nomination of Mr. Ramsey Holmsteed as ambassador to France was introduced by Senator Baukin, the Chairman of the Senate Foreign Relations Committee, Senator Hoots threatened all manner of legislative sleights of hand, including a filibuster, in order to stop the nomination. The use of procedural minutiae to sidetrack the nomination of a highly qualified public servant has become the hallmark of the North Carolina Republican, and bodes ill for the committee should the Republicans ever gain control of the senate.'"

Wiley hated the *Post.* In fact, he hated most newspapers. He felt that they, along with university faculties, were part of a liberal, secularist conspiracy trying to destroy American values. On occasion I tried to get the senator to give me a clean singular definition of "American Values," but he never would. I finally understood why—the best definition was the one the listener came up with. Wiley didn't have to give a definition because no matter what he said it wouldn't satisfy everybody, so he let each voter decide what was meant by American Values.

My father once told me a story about a meeting he arranged between a candidate for governor and a local committee of party operatives. It was in the early sixties and the civil rights movement was the primary topic of discussion in our part of the state. While the state was predominately Democratic, the eastern North Carolina version of the party was a great deal more conservative and racially divided than that in the rest of the state, especially in the large urban centers. During the meeting, one of the men present said to the candidate, "Mr. So and So, I just want to know where you stand on. . . . you know."

Without blinking and with a steady gaze at the questioner, the candidate said, "I think you know where I stand on that issue." Silence. Then the questioner said, "I thought so, but we just had to know for sure."

Obfuscation is the elixir of smart politicians.

⌒

Wiley continued his ranting. "And you know what really scrapes my carrot, Billy? What really does it, is the fact that if it hadn't been for President Reagan's hard line, the damn Russkies would still be carving up the world, and here we are trying to send Walter Mitty to France." Wiley rubbed his cheek and looked back at the paper. "I got half a mind to just stand up and tell 'em, 'You boys stupid enough to nominate him? You got 'im. And you deserve 'im. And the frogs deserve him as well.' If we're gonna play our second team, it might as well be with the frogs."

Wiley was like a symphony tuning up. The longer he played, the louder he got. No point in doing anything but nodding and letting him get all his practicing out.

"What time did you get home last night?" he asked, "You look like you was scraped off the bottom of the pot."

I had hoped that I looked better than I felt. "Actually, Senator, I think I'm coming down with a little cold. I wasn't late last night . . . ten or eleven." An easy lie; not even a stretch. So I was off by three hours. In Washington that's a close approximation.

Wiley put the paper down and turned toward the wall behind his desk. With a faint smile, he gazed at the rows of framed editorial cartoons, staged handshakes and hugs, honorary degrees and letters from famous and not-so-famous persons. The not-so-famous letters were characteristically fawning missives that made Wiley feel like a savior of the common man.

"You know, Billy, I was thinking about what you guys were discussing yesterday. All that stuff about fighting battles, and tough talk versus profile ads and sweet smiles." He looked over at me. "John's got a point, son. I know he can be a bit bossy and uppity sometimes, but he knows what he's talking about. You need to swallow a little pride and listen up."

I nodded ever so slightly. It was all I'd give him. "I'm sure you're right, Senator. I'll count to twenty next time, not just ten."

Wiley looked back at his ego wall. "Listen, I like the profile piece. It tells folks what we're really about. My daddy raised us as straight-talking Christian people, and I ain't afraid to claim it." He looked back me. "But he raised us to be swords as well as plowshares. Plowshares are good, but they don't win the battles we're forced to fight these days. You remember the walking staff, Billy?" I nodded. "It taught me that life doesn't allow slackers and weaklings to lead the parade."

He stood up, straightening his back. The flag standing behind his desk fluttered as Wiley swept back his arm. "Men, and lots of 'em, have died for that flag, William. The red in those stripes is from the blood of courage shed on the fields of battle. To honor it requires the solidarity of men of character. Men who know what duty is.

"Men far removed from such as Randolph James. I don't like it; I didn't ask for it, but I am a sword for this country . . . a sword at war with the nay-sayers and socialists. Billy, John's right. We need to hit 'em. We need to hit 'em hard. We need to show the apologizers and the liberals what courage and dedication mean. We need to show the country what cowardly Holmsteed-liberal ways mean. There'll be time for plowshares when the work is done." He turned toward his wall and stood silent for a few seconds.

"Hoover told me about those partial-birth abortion pictures, and I suppose he's right. I suppose. Billy, folks look to me for the truth, regardless of consequences or . . . or image. I'm charged to remind our people that there are those out there dangerous to our way of life. People who put man ahead of God."

He jerked his head around. His face was frozen into hard lines. His lips were tight and straight, and his color was high. His eyes were slits and anger ran down his cheeks. He usually kept this part of himself, the mean part, hidden, but "hidden" was the operative word; the meanness was always there, unchanging and righteous, a mass of human bile, ready to vent like magma in its own mysterious time. He stood like this for a while, hard to say exactly how long, and then, very slowly, he began to cool. The sword sheathed himself. But I believe he saw the worried look on my face, because he then smiled as though his outburst had never happened.

"When I got home last night, I re-read a letter from my daughter Betsy. I remembered it while driving over here. It could be something we might use. It could be the punch John's talking about. Read it and tell me what you think."

Wiley handed the letter to me then sat down and resumed reading the *Post*.

I never warmed to Betsy Graham. She and Wiley had been at odds for a long time. He had told me about some of their differences while she was growing up, but recently things seemed to improve. I think Betsy finally realized that Wiley was her big meal ticket and that her Pillsbury dough-boy of a husband wasn't taking her to any promised land. Harvey was a CPA with a fair-sized regional accounting firm in Raleigh, but Betsy realized that that was a life sentence, not a career. He would be there until the day he retired. She, on the other hand, was restless.

Over the past few years she had begun to position herself in Raleigh as a leader in the evangelical born-again community. She began to conduct prayer sessions and hold Bible study groups, some of which were so large that they were held in the Raleigh convention center. She and a select group of women started a retail outlet specializing in religious items for the home or garden. A small publishing house was soon incorporated. And all of this was done as Betsy Hoots Graham. If she could, she would have ditched the Graham and just used her maiden name. The Hoots brand was something she'd come to cherish and she wasn't about to let it slide. If she could keep Daddy on the evening news and the front pages of the papers, her star would continue to rise. Thank you, Jesus.

I read her letter carefully and remember thinking; 'a derelict urinating on the head of another derelict passed out against a crumbling wall, Lucy Sue would love this. She'd probably hang it in her living room over the mantelpiece.' I re-read the letter and with the proper look of indignation said, "Doesn't sound like something the NEA should be funding, Senator."

"Our grasp of the obvious is impressive, Billy. Find out what the hell is going on over there and what those pointy-headed bastards are up to."

I got up and folded the letter into my coat pocket. "Senator, I'll call Carl Fanceler. He and I were at Chapel Hill together; he's currently the Assistant Director for Development and Alumni Affairs at Carolina. He'll check this out for us."

Wiley looked back up from his paper and smiled. "Let me know, and make sure to get hold of Hugh Crutcher this morning. If he gives you a problem, call me. I'll remind the ingrate about past favors. We need some money, Billy."

⁓

I walked back to my office and closed the door. I needed quiet and a double dose of Advil. I sat down, then spread Betsy's letter out on my desk. I wondered whether it really could be the basis for a new hardline ad. After all, it was just an art show on a college campus. Who the hell is gonna get worked up about that? How large an audience would that exhibition draw, anyway? Whatever the deal, I needed to find out what this was all about. I rang Ruth Lee.

"Ruth Lee, if you would, please get Carl Fanceler on the phone for me. Do you have . . . okay, fine. Yes, at work first. Thanks, and ring me when you get him."

Carl and I had had a typical college friendship: a few classes together, the occasional party, promises to stay in touch, all the while knowing that neither of us would make the effort. And we probably wouldn't have if Carl hadn't decided to change his life by leaving his banking job in Charlotte and moving back to Chapel Hill, and if I hadn't gone to work for a man the university wanted to stay close to. So Carl pretended to be a better friend than he knew he was, and I, needing information and favors from the university from time to time, did the same. It helped us both. I got a channel into the school and Carl got a direct line into the office of Senator Wiley Grace Hoots.

Ruth Lee buzzed my phone. "Yes?"

"Mr. Fanceler is on the phone." I closed my eyes and pictured Carl.

"Carl, how they hanging, bubba?" *They* were probably hanging on a chain around his wife's neck. Having met the lovely Mrs. Fanceler, I was, in fact, sure of it. Carl's banking career had been going nowhere and the Mrs. figured his chances for a big title and a well-heeled retirement was better at Carolina than at NationsBank, so she got him to quit the bank as soon as he was hired at Carolina. She orchestrated the whole process and was probably right to do so.

As the Assistant Director of Development and Alumni Affairs, Carl was just a heartbeat away from being director, and considering the age and health of Elliot Schaeffer, a heartbeat was pretty close. Elliot had been at the school since Adam stood upright and got tar on his heels while walking around in the Garden of Eden, which, in North Carolina, they call Chapel Hill. He would die in the job unless some eager chancellor managed to retire him, which seemed unlikely given his popularity with the alumni, at least the older affluent alumni.

"Not bad, Billy. Elliot and I are, as usual, trying to raise money for the school to replace the constant drain of funds proposed by the state. It's a never-ending struggle, but then I don't need to tell you about the challenge of government funding, do I?"

"No sir, you sure don't. If it makes you feel any better, the state of North Carolina is one hell of a lot better off than the federal government. At least we have to balance our budget in North Carolina." We were either going to continue this inane line of conversation or I needed to move to the subject at hand. Fortunately, my subject could now ride in on that budgeting segue.

"Speaking of federal and state funding, Carl, Betsy Graham, Wiley's daughter, sent him a letter describing an art show at the Ackland that was paid for by the National Endowment for the Arts along with, of course, the state of North Carolina as represented by the university. Apparently, she and her husband were in Chapel Hill visiting their daughter and went to the Ackland to see an Old Masters prints show. On the way out, they happened to go through some galleries displaying paintings they were none too pleased with. You know anything about this show?"

The silence was deafening. I could just imagine the sweat beads jumping out on Carl's forehead. His brain must be in overload. I threw him a life saver.

"Carl, I assume you don't know the particulars, but what have you heard? Is this a big deal? Have you heard any scuttlebutt about it? Any waves crashing over Alumni Affairs because of it?"

Carl waited a moment longer. "Uh, no, not that I know of." He mumbled something else, then added, "You kind of caught me off guard, Billy. I had to think about what she might have seen, but now that I think about it, I do recall hearing about a show she might be referring to. I haven't read a review of it in the *Daily Tar Heel* or any of the local papers, but my next-door neighbor is a prof in the fine arts department and he was talking about a recent NEA grant and what a big deal it was for the department. I don't remember anything he said about the exhibit except that it was well received by the NEA and the panel that selected the art.

"Why? What has the senator heard?"

"He hasn't heard anything, Carl. Like I said, his daughter Betsy and her husband saw the show and reported to him that it had some very disturbing art in it. Something about a man urinating on another man. The kind of thing academics go for these days, political correctness run amok. You know, 'It isn't their fault that they urinate on each other. They had a lousy childhood, forced to eat food with too much sugar or fat or whatever.' Anyway, I need to find out about the show and who paid for what. You got any ideas?"

I really didn't enjoy pulling Carl's chain this hard. His breathing told me he was in full-scale panic mode, and that he wanted to get as far away from this as possible.

"Billy, I'm on it. Let me call Evan Lee, the director of the Ackland, and see what this is all about. I may have him call you . . . if that's okay?"

"Sure, Carl. Give him my office number here as well as our offices in Raleigh. I'm going to be spending a fair amount of time in the state with the election so close."

"Okay, thanks, Billy. I'll get back to you, or better yet, I'll have Dr. Lee call. He'll have more information than I, and I'm sure can answer all your questions. We'll track this down for the senator—no problem."

I could hear the relief in Carl's voice believing that he had just handed off this headache.

6.

My intercom buzzed. Ruth Lee, in her most acerbate, pre-coffee voice, informed me that a Dr. Lee from somewhere in Chapel Hill was on the line 5.

"Dr. Lee, how nice to hear from you. Carl said you might be calling. First, let me say that I'm a great fan of your museum. Except to enjoy the museum's air conditioning on hot spring or early fall days, I didn't often darken your door step while a student; however, I've enjoyed many of your exhibits in the—more than I like to think—years since. You may not remember, but I met you a year ago at the opening of the medieval exhibit you did in conjunction with the museum at Duke. I was there with Lucy Sue Tribble from Raleigh and Charles Wilson from UNC's history department."

I had, in fact, been to a fair number of exhibits at the museum over the years, so it wasn't just kissing ass to say so. The Ackland was a small museum by national standards but had an outstanding reputation within museum circles, especially academic museum circles. It wasn't the Fogg at Harvard but then few others were.

Director for at least a dozen years, Evan Lee had the reputation of being both a serious academic and a pragmatist, operating in the real world under real-world rules. Unlike many academics who seemed to love tweaking the jowls of legislators, especially conservative ones, Evan had developed a finely honed talent for kissing rather than biting the hand that fed him. Thus, after a few more minutes of polite conversation and a number of disingenuous compliments to me and the senator, Evan got to the point.

"Billy, I understand from Carl that Senator Hoots' daughter, Mrs. Graham, recently came through the museum and, in particular, an exhibit entitled, 'The World View of Xers.' I can't say that I am entirely surprised at what I assume were her reactions to some of the work in the show, but she may not have read the information about the show before she entered. At one point, I told our curators that no one should enter except through a single room and that a proper explanation of the show should be displayed in that room, but I didn't follow up on that direction. Now we have a situation that could have been avoided. I take the blame for not following up."

"Evan, knowing Mrs. Graham, I'm not sure any explanation could have satisfied her, but the senator has asked me to look into the show. I'm going to be in Raleigh next week and thought that perhaps I could come by for a few minutes and see the show and get some idea of what Mrs. Graham is talking about."

"That would be fine, Billy, but unfortunately we have already taken it down."

"Well, then maybe you could explain it to me? I'm sure it was a well-documented exhibit, being an NEA-funded show."

"Very well documented. In fact, if you would like, I could have our chief curator, Dr. Ginna Humphreys, take you through a quick slide presentation of the show. She is very proud of receiving NEA funding and equally proud of the outstanding reviews we received. I think you'll be impressed. If it isn't too much trouble, I think we would need about an hour to go through the whole evolution of the show. Is that okay?"

I agreed—knowing that the presentation would be interesting but pointless. Wiley didn't give a damn about the content or background of the exhibit; he wanted to know just how offensive it really was and whether there was anything in the show that could be helpful to his campaign.

As usual, it was my job to arrange the bout and take the punches, so I could report back as to the strength of our opponent. While the university wasn't usually thought of as an opponent, to Wiley they almost always were. After being with the senator for a few years, I finally came to the conclusion that his animosity toward Chapel Hill wasn't because he had been turned down there as a student, though that had to play a part, rather it was the condescending way in which the administrators and professors treated him whenever he was in their presence. He always said to me, prior to a meeting with anyone from the university, "Get ready to be stonewalled and pissed on, Billy." He at least kept his most vituperative remarks about Carolina at a minimum around me.

Per my suggestion, we scheduled a meeting for the following week. Five o'clock in Dr. Lee's office at the Ackland. This gave me an excuse to arrange an evening with Lucy, starting with dinner at my favorite Chapel Hill restaurant. The prospect of spending time with Ms. Tribble made whatever pain may come from a visit to the museum bearable.

⌒

Evan Lee hurried across the gallery floor. He was wearing a pair of pressed khakis and an elderly herringbone sports coat with leather patches on the elbows. His oversized bow tie featured a day-glo floral pattern that matched neither the color nor the design of his jacket. This threw his look off center, like painting a Picasso head on a Rembrandt body.

"Hello, Evan, it's good to see you. I appreciate your taking the time to see me . . . love your tie."

"Thanks, my daughter gave it to me a few years ago. It's sort of expressionistic, don't you think?"

"Just what I was about to say."

Evan looked at his watch. "I told Dr. Humphreys to come to my office. We need to move on."

We entered Dr. Lee's office and closed the door. He settled in the large chair behind his desk, and I sat on the small two-seat sofa against the wall to his left. Sitting there in his high-back brown leather chair, Evan gave every appearance of an owl looking out of its burrow in some ancient oak tree. I, sitting on the small sofa, arms spread across its back, looked like and definitely felt like a seated crucifix.

"Evan, I don't want to cause any concern, but I do need to understand the facts around this show. As you know, Senator Hoots has had his differences with the folks over at the NEA. I personally think they do a pretty good job, but contemporary art in whatever form is hard for a lot of people to understand and accept. I've gotta admit that a lot of modern stuff leaves me kind of cold. I get the feeling that some of it is out there just to provoke folks and cause an argument. I bet you know a number of your associates here at Chapel Hill who say and write things just to cause a stir." Evan smiled, tacitly agreeing.

"I understand, Billy, but this show is not about causing a stir or making people mad. It's about giving young artists a chance to showcase their work. These are not academics, but a group of young folks who are serious about their art. They were chosen from among hundreds of young artists nominated by experts from universities as well as museums and various art publications. Each artist submitted a portfolio of their work for judging by our national panel. You'll see."

Evan was clearly passionate about this show, but it was equally clear to me that Wiley would probably look at it like it was just another bunch of academics yanking his chain.

Someone knocked on the door, but before Evan could respond Dr. Ginna Humphreys was in the room. I looked up and for an embarrassingly long time didn't move. I just sat there, probably with my mouth open, staring. Ginna Humphreys was beautiful, not what one expects in a chief curator. Chief curators are frumpy-looking, thin women with thick glasses and straight uncombed hair, or maybe hair mounted on their head in an old-lady bun. Ginna was full figured, five feet eight, probably one hundred and twenty pounds, and brunette. She had the most beautiful green eyes I have ever seen. "Billy, may I introduce Dr. Ginna Humphreys, my chief curator." I managed to get to my feet, closed my mouth, and stuck out my hand.

"Doctor, I'm William Bowater, Senator Wiley Hoots' chief administrative assistant. From one chief to another, it's a pleasure to meet you."

"Thank you, Mr. Bowater, and thank you for coming to the museum. I look forward to telling you about 'The World View of Xers.' Perhaps you can help the senator to understand that this is a serious show, nothing to regret or be ashamed of."

"First, my name is Billy. Mr. Bowater is my father. Next, I'm sure that it is or was a serious show. Please, you don't need to apologize for anything. I look forward to seeing the work."

"Billy, Ginna has a slide projector set up in the conference room next door so why don't we move in there and put some meat on the bones."

In the conference room, a slide projector on the long table was directed at a white board on the wall. Ginna stood by the board and Evan took a chair at the table, motioning me to take the chair next to him. I looked at my watch, not to see the time but to make sure they knew this could not be an unending lecture.

Ginna recounted the weeks and months of planning, budgeting, and re-budgeting. She described their discussions on rationale, composition, methods of judging, and the strategies necessary to encourage both institutional and individual contributions. It was clear that the exhibit had been not only a project of passion for her and the museum staff, but a critical and intellectual success; however, I needed more specific information.

I smiled and slowly held up my hand. "Ginna, this is fascinating and clearly this was an exhibit in which you and your staff take great pride; however, I am here because Senator Hoots received some comments about works of art that didn't exactly seem to him to meet the criteria for inclusion in a school art exhibit. Something about urination and blasphemy was mentioned. What was all that about?"

The smile that had painted Ginna's face only moments before was now gone. "Okay, I see. The senator's real interest has nothing to do with art or education; rather, he is looking for a way to punish or criticize the university."

How could I be so stupid. I should have seen this coming and left the urination and blasphemy out until they occurred in her presentation. I groped for a way out.

"Dr. Humphreys, I'm sorry. That was foolish of me; however, bad timing aside, I thought you knew that I had come because someone wrote to Senator Hoots complaining about the subject matter of some of the works. I didn't mean to diminish your presentation, so please go on with my apologies."

The smile, with something less than full sincerity, returned to her face.

"Billy, I didn't mean to be so snappy, but as you said, this was a project that was very important to me and the museum staff. I realize that you're here at the senator's direction because of some criticisms made to him about the show. So, without further delay, let me quickly run through some slides which will highlight the exhibit and hopefully provide you with enough information so that you, in turn, can assure the senator that we are serious people who had no intention of offending anyone.

"I'm going to discuss the artists as they appear in the catalogue. There's no rationale for the order other than random selection. As I mentioned earlier, the jury picked ten artists for 'The World View of Xers' show, six men and four women. While painting was the predominant medium, sculpture, photography, and print making were also represented. First slide, please, Evan."

One after the other, in an impressive parade of shapes and colors, the slides of the artists' work filled the screen. Ginna's commentary covered the individual artist's background, the rationale of the jury in picking the work, and the unique talent or vision that each artist brought to the show.

While I clearly was not an expert in visual arts, I had been in Washington long enough to have gotten a better-than-average exposure to the diversity and dynamics of contemporary painting and sculpture. Most of the work was what Wiley would term "Modern," which is to say, abstract. It was non-representational, using forms and colors to convey emotion. Not until the work of the eighth artist came up did the show become at all representational. Ginna paused before calling for the next slide.

"The next artist is undoubtedly the most controversial of the show, the one who painted the work that Mrs. Graham referred to in her letter. I also happen to believe that he is without question the most talented. His name is Christian Pope, and he is a twenty-something-year-old black man who lives in Washington, D.C. Mr. Pope has played it very close to the vest when it comes to sharing personal data, but the faculty at American University, who nominated him, are very keen on his work. He has been a student there for over three years, and in that time, has produced an impressive body of work. I suspect that Christian Pope is a pseudonym; however, Mr. Pope insists that it is his real name. In any case, he is an exceptional painter. Next slide, please."

"This first picture is entitled *Jordan's Water.*" She made no further comment since she clearly knew that the painting spoke for itself and that I would probably prefer to look and ponder without distraction. If that was her motivation, it was correct.

The painting was perhaps four feet wide by six feet high. The frame was simple and plain; the images were not. Betsy Graham's description had been accurate as far as subject matter, but, not surprisingly, had not mentioned the astounding impact the images had on the viewer. I can't remember whether my mouth dropped open while looking at the slide, but my mind did. It was captivating and clearly worthy of being shown in any gallery in the world. Christian Pope would be a name, regardless of Wiley's protestations, that would become known throughout the country.

"Well, Evan, I wouldn't say Mrs. Graham's description was inaccurate but I would say that she didn't give the quality of the painting the credit it deserves. The questions that will arise are ones that I'm sure you can imagine without me mentioning them."

"Billy, there is no doubt that this is a strong image, but let me try and put it into context. Mr. Pope was raised in Washington, D.C., in that part of the city not shown on the post cards sold at the Smithsonian gift shop. As you can see, his Washington is a crumbling, decaying shell of a city, hardly the pride of a grateful nation. Where the image is taken from really doesn't matter, though; it could be anywhere—Chicago, New York, L.A., it's irrelevant.

The painting personifies poverty, hopelessness, and human degradation. If the fallen buildings and urban ruin don't make the point, then the central image of a man urinating on another, probably unconscious, man certainly does. So what is this? Some strange rite? Some gang ritual? Or is this simply the perverted, devaluing way of life in a place that has lost all hope and human decency?

"We can't tell, but look on the wall of the building immediately behind the two men. How extraordinary! An urban mural, one of many such projects done on the walls of American inner cities during the sixties and seventies, is cast as a background to the sordid events of the street. Billy, I don't know if you recognize the painting, or at least the painting from which the mural is copied, but it is one of the most famous medieval religious masterpieces ever done. The original work was by Andrea del Verrocchio, the teacher of DaVinci, and is titled 'The Baptism of Christ'; however, as you can see, in Mr. Pope's version, Jesus and John the Baptist are standing in the river Jordan, kissing. I don't think I need to point out that this was not the case in del Verrocchio's."

I held up my hand. "Evan, I get it. I didn't know the del Verrocchio painting, but one doesn't need to know the exact artist or period to understand the significance. Its old and it's of a sacred subject. Enough said."

But I also knew that the images, symbols, and the idea of Christ kissing another man on the mouth would be a tough sell for Wiley. Let me rephrase that, I could just as well try to explain relativity to a parrot. Evan tapped on the table to rouse me.

"Billy, you seem deep in thought. Can I help?"

"I'm thinking about my conversation with Wiley . . . Senator Hoots.

He is not famous for a long attention span, so repeating Ginna's preface, enlightening as it was, is out. I can explain that this is a show done by young artists, individuals in roughly the same age bracket as his granddaughter. He doesn't understand his granddaughter, so that will make sense.

"But I'm getting bogged down somewhere between rebellious youth and a picture of one wino pissing on another who is laying on the ground in front of a painting showing Jesus Christ tongue-kissing John the Baptist. That transition's going to be tricky."

Evan rubbed his thumb and forefinger across the corners of his mouth and began again. "Billy, this show is not about insulting people. It is about letting young, talented artists express themselves without restrictions. These are young men and women who feel deeply about their craft; who feel deeply about their lives. Most of this work is technically sound but lacking in maturity and sophistication of concept. Some is contrived and youthfully naive, but that's the point.

"Young artists have to experiment; they must work to grow, and offering them a venue and a financial reward motivates them to push their work to higher levels. They need the pressure of meeting a deadline and being in a competition in order to expand their technique and composition.

"Mr. Pope is different. He is more mature, and while he says that he is in his mid-to late twenties, I suspect he is probably at the north end of the Xers age scale—maybe in his mid-thirties. What you see in his paintings are life experiences drawn from a well out of which no one should have to drink. Pain may not always be necessary for the production of great art, but I have come to believe that most genius has flowed from a tortured soul."

He was probably right, but I also knew that such philosophizing would be lost on Wiley. Wiley saw the world as black or white. To him there is good and bad; right and wrong; true and false, and these are all laid out in great detail in the Christian Bible. Within that Bible there is a quote to soothe every soul looking for justification. Wiley says that the search for truth by the young need venture only as far as a Baptist

Sunday school. I knew that that search is not likely to encounter urination, homosexuality, or salvation for drunken sinners.

The fact that the university, to Wiley a collection of "pointy heads,"
and the NEA, another bunch of arrogant academics, had worked together on this show would mean that two of his least favorite institutions had colluded to produce a disgusting and sacrilegious show to
insult visitors' eyes and souls. He might see this as his big chance to
kill two birds with one stone, or at least wound one and kill the other.
He could kill the NEA by issuing a terminal legislative edict against its
funding, and wound the university by splashing this show all over the
papers in North Carolina, thus, inflaming legislators and voters against
such liberal blasphemous rubbish. I also imagined that he would have
little trouble using two "deviates," as he was so fond of calling gays, as
grist in his campaign mill.

I could already picture the campaign line: Public money used to
blaspheme. *Your* money to blaspheme. What has happened to family
values? Where is the respect for society? Shit, the potential rhetoric
was endless. No matter that this show didn't count a whit among the
issues that really needed talking about, it was the kind of values-thing
that John Carter could wallow in.

This was the requisite punch in the gut to that group of voters most
coveted by Carter & Horton. And having absorbed the punch, they'd
react with fury—and they'd come running, cudgels raised, out of their
caves to vote.

Ginna cleared her throat to get my attention. She was in a hurry to
finish, but she did not want to end with *Jordan's Water.*

"I have one more artist to show you. This is the work of a woman by
the name of Aeriel Sopwith, and as you can see, it represents a totally
different attitude about the world than that of Mr. Pope. Aeriel is an
optimist, a celebrant in life's parade, and her work reflects her exhila-
ration. Her photographs gather the human form into a world that her
audience can understand. The hands, feet, human form, all of it weaves
a tale that is wonderful to see.

"It has always amazed Aeriel that some people find her photography to be obscene or tasteless, and she often wonders how something as natural and beautiful as the naked figure of a human being can be viewed in such a cynical way. What is it about the human body that makes its owners so nervous? Why is the human body so reviled, when revealed?

"In these last few slides, Billy, Aeriel depicts, in black and white, two adolescent girls. One image amongst the trees, another with the girls reclining, several photos by a stream, and finally a picture of the two girls laughing and embracing under a waterfall. You can see the kinetic waters shining off the bodies of the girls and the liquid reflections of their skin mirrored in the agitated surface of the pool in which they're standing. It is a photograph of unbridled joy and motion."

She was right, but seen through the eyes of Wiley Hoots, these images would be interpreted not as a celebration of joy and motion but rather a crass attempt to titillate the pedophilic inclinations of other artists with similar sexual tendencies.

Evan turned the projector off and reached over his shoulder and flipped on the overhead lights. I checked my watch, then waited for Ginna to sit down. They both waited for me to say something.

What worried me the most was the fact that I couldn't think of a strategy against Carter's strategy. The exhibit was a fact; the paintings and photographs were a fact; the NEA was one of the sponsors; the university displayed the show on public property; and freedom of speech, while protected, wouldn't in this case be respected. I knew John well enough to know how he would use this; I just didn't yet know what to say back.

I finally put on my best good-ole-boy smile and said, "Well, I think it's safe to say that little of the art in this show will be understood by the senator. It is also safe to say that neither of these last two artists is going to be easy to explain to Wiley or probably most other North Carolinians. Neither artist produces stuff that the average person would understand or appreciate. I'm not being judgmental here, only realistic. I'm gonna have to think about this and how I want to position it to the senator. I am comfortable with the ideas of Generation X and youthful exuberance, and learning by experimenting, but I'm not sure how to explain or at least position the NEA and the university to him. Actually, I think Wiley will understand the university's position. He doesn't agree with most of the things the university does anyway, so this will just be more of the same to him.

"What I am concerned about is the use of NEA funds. Wiley wouldn't fund the NEA at all if he had his way, so this will just be more ammunition for him. You might remember a quote attributed to the Senator, 'I don't care if you want to draw dirty pictures on the bathroom wall, just don't ask me to buy the crayons for you.' He got a lot of laughs with that, but the fact is, he meant it.

"Wiley doesn't feel that the government has any business support- ing 'the arts.' I'm not saying that I agree with him but as I have said, what I believe doesn't matter. He's the senator. I'll do what I can to downplay the show and perhaps we can move the campaign to more large-scale, substantive issues. In any case, I appreciate your taking the time to ex- plain this to me and for what it's worth, I like the show."

Ginna and Evan stood up, but their expressions told me they feared they hadn't succeeded in convincing me of the show's value.

"Guys, don't look so worried. I understand what you are saying and I promise I'll try and move the campaign to other subjects, but under- stand, I'm the assistant. I assist. No one really is asking me to define policy or campaign strategy. It's Senator Hoots who counts here, not me."

The minute the words came out of my mouth I could feel my spit drying up. How easily the lies flowed. I had just been thinking about how John Carter would use this show, knowing that I had little chance of stopping him. Yet I still promised what I knew would be impossible. No, John Carter would climb on the NEA, the university, and especially those two poor artists like a pit bull on a meat wagon, and I could only make a nominal attempt to pull him off.

I stood up, smiled, and shook hands all around. "I'll be in touch, Evan. Ginna, it was a real pleasure and congratulations on a great show." I took the two catalogues offered by Evan and walked out of the small conference room and into the galleries of the Ackland. I thought to myself, *Take a deep breath, Billy. Look around and remember what this place meant to you. Maybe you can move the campaign away. Maybe you can be Huck on the raft, lying to the bounty hunters looking for runaway slaves. Maybe you can do the right thing, painful as it might be to your legislative career. Maybe you can be the best part of a Bowater.* Maybe my head hurt. Maybe I didn't want to think anymore. Maybe I wanted to just go blank, to be invisible. But I definitely wanted the expectation ghosts to evaporate and leave me alone.

7.

"You know something, I don't give a damn what Senator Evans thinks about my stand on foreign aid. He is entitled to his opinion, but when he says that the American people support the idea of sending their hard-earned tax money to those socialist you-know-whats, I'm not going to just sit there and nod in agreement when I know it isn't so." Wiley was not having a good day, and he wasn't helping the person on the other end of the line have one either.

I was in my office on the far side of the reception room but could hear every word. They could probably hear every word in the Hart Building next door. The Foreign Relations Committee was the most frustrating of Wiley's assignments. He loved the exposure and prestige of the committee, but he felt isolated and alone—there weren't enough good conservatives serving with him. By this, Wiley meant no other members felt that the U.S. should invade Cuba, that foreign aid was a waste of money, that the U.N. should be disbanded, and that we should close our embassy in Beijing and cut all trade alliances with mainland China.

I looked at my watch. It was time for my morning briefing with Wiley. We had a pretty light schedule for the day, only one committee meeting, but there were a few campaign items that we needed to discuss. I would have preferred him to be in a better mood, though.

"Senator? You got a few minutes?

Wiley looked up, "Come on in, Billy. I need to be at an agriculture working group on the Smitherman proposal in thirty minutes, that enough time?"

"Yes, sir. In fact, I was just going to remind you of that. As usual, you're ahead of me. Sir, there are a few schedule items I want to discuss concerning the campaign that . . ."

"Did you ever talk to that friend of yours in Chapel Hill about that art show Betsy wrote me about?" I had wanted to bring this up as a throwaway item at the end.

"I talked to Betsy this weekend and she went on again about that art thing. I think . . ."

I held up my hand. "Senator, don't worry. I'm on top of it. In fact, I spent an hour last week at the museum in Chapel Hill with the director, Dr. Evan Lee, as well as his chief curator, a Dr. Ginna Humphreys."

Wiley leaned back in his chair and crossed his arms. "And?"

"And I believe I have a full understanding of the show. Basically it is or was—it's not up anymore—an exhibit done by a younger generation of artists, called Generation X. This would roughly be people between eleven and thirty. The post-baby-boomer generation. In any case, the young artists in the show were selected by a large number of museum directors, art critics, and art professors." Wiley smirked. "It appears that the preparation, selection process, and professionalism of the university were thorough. They are proud of the show and it got some positive reviews. But being a contemporary exhibit would by definition mean that it may not be for everyone."

"You mean me," Wiley said.

"Well, sir, many others too, but . . . yes, sir, I mean you." There was no point trying to get philosophical about this. Like I had told Ginna and Evan, Senator Hoots is going to find this very difficult to understand much less accept, and I had no intention of trying to educate him in the subtleties of modern art.

"They do a catalogue?"

"Yes, sir."

"You got one?"

"Yes, sir."

He gave me a 'so where the hell is it' look. "Am I gonna have to beg for it?"

"No, sir. I have one in my office. Let me get it."

"You do that."

Wiley by this time knew me pretty well. He could tell I was uncomfortable with the whole subject. I was always uncomfortable when he started on a rampage against Chapel Hill. Not that I was the most gung-ho of alumni, but I did have a sense of loyalty to the place. I was, after all, a Morehead Scholar, which is to say that the university, via the Morehead Foundation, had paid for my entire education for four years. And it wasn't as if my family couldn't pay the cost, clearly they could and would have, but to be nominated for and then receive a Morehead was a big deal and a great honor, something that William Jr. could and did brag about to anyone who would listen. The fact that it saved him a few bucks was also okay. I loved my time at the university, both as an undergraduate and a law student, but I didn't bleed Carolina blue like some. In any case, I would try to protect the university and its show as far as I could without losing my credibility with Wiley. I'm not a total whore, frequent evidence to the contrary, so with catalogue in hand I returned to Wiley's office. As I crossed the reception area, I kept saying to myself, *No sir, ain't no niggers on this raft, just my pap, and he got— uhm—we needs a tow.* I was the one needin' a tow. I needed to Huck up and help my friends.

"Here it is. May I suggest . . ."

"Just let me see it, Billy."

"Yes, sir." I put the catalogue on his desk and returned to my chair. For the next five minutes, Wiley thumbed through the book, occasionally stopping and shaking his head. Finally, he looked up, "I just don't get it, Billy. Why would someone who clearly has the talent to paint something beautiful, paint such a disgusting, vile mockery of the Lord? Even if this Mr. Pope, or whatever his blasphemous name is, isn't a Christian, and you can be sure that he isn't, why trash someone else's beliefs? What were those arrogant bastards in Chapel Hill thinking about?

"But why am I even asking? They were thinking about getting money from those perverts at the NEA so they could publish some pompous, pseudo-intellectual catalogue and send it to their buddies at the other universities to show how brilliant they are."

He flipped the catalogue over to me and then stared at me. I kept his gaze but didn't say anything. If I tried to guess what he was thinking or where he wanted to go with this, I could be wrong and thus dig myself a deep hole. Better to wait. He would tell me what he was thinking, what he wanted. He probably couldn't wait.

"So, what do we do with this?" he finally asked, looking from me to his ego wall. "How do we use this to point out the dangers of a government that seeks to impose its socialist agenda on the nation? On well-meaning people who don't even see it coming?"

He wasn't speaking to me. He was wearing his public-face and speaking, as if they were standing before him, to those dozen or so letter writers whose unctuous missives were framed on his wall. Those voters who had raised him in his own mind to sainthood. By believing that "they" don't see it coming, he had put himself in the position of both shepherd and prophet. It was up to him to protect them . . . to save them from the evil in the world that they couldn't see or understand. He finally turned and looked directly at me and said, "What do we do with it? How do we use this without hurting ourselves?"

I rubbed my chin, borrowing time, and said, "Well, sir, I've thought a lot about that and there are several things I believe we need to consider. First, I don't think the university administration was aware of the show, but I do think they'll defend it on the grounds of academic freedom if we bring the matter up. Second, I think Governor James could be put in the difficult position of defending the university should we choose to put him there, but are people really going to blame Governor James for an art exhibit at Carolina? After all, he went to State, not Carolina.

"Third, I'm not sure that attacking the university will win many points with the majority of our target voters or our target contributors. We have a lot of support from Carolina alumni. In fact, I would guess that Carolina alums give the majority of our money. Finally, I don't think most people even know what or who the NEA is and thus don't have an ax to grind with them. In summary, I think it's a risk, even a distraction from issues more appealing to our voters and contributors."

Wiley had been staring at the top of his desk. When I finished, he looked up and smiled. "Billy, when has it ever been a problem for me to take a risk? Those stuffy bastards at Carolina have pissed off enough people in this state to deserve a little heat, and the NEA doesn't have a friend among real Americans, just the hoity-toity liberal crowd. Besides, the NEA is the federal government and the federal government, as President Reagan said, is the problem.

"But just for a minute let's say you're right and we might needlessly anger some Carolina alums. Who says that we have to be the ones to attack the university and the NEA in the first place? Who says that we can't simply react to a national outcry over this foul and sacrilegious show?"

He wasn't asking questions that he expected answers to; he was setting me up. He was putting me to a test for which he already had the answers. I played along.

"So, if we stand back and don't make a big deal about this show, who will?"

He shook his head. "Billy, Billy, get that class A mind of yours in the game. Where are we going at the end of the month?"

Actually, I was a little embarrassed that I hadn't thought of it. A solution that would give me cover and hopefully keep the heat on the NEA rather than on the university and the artists. A real conscience cleanser. I smiled and said, "New Orleans. The Christian Crusade. Earl Anthony and the biggest mailing list in America. Brilliant, Senator."

Wiley just rocked back in his chair and smiled.

8.

I've never liked Earl Anthony or maybe I've never respected him. I used to believe that the spiritual shepherds among us were from stouter timber than we—that they were here to guide us by example. I know now that that's yet another Sunday-school myth passed down sometime during confirmation training; not too hard to fool a twelve year old.

About eight o'clock one night, during my weekly indoctrination, we had finished rehearsing a play and I was chosen to take the costumes back to the storage room in the basement of the church. As I was coming upstairs from the basement, I heard what sounded like a frightened cry, a woman in trouble. It wasn't exactly "O God," a supplication I have since learned has nothing at all to do with prayer, rather, it was more like OH OH OH, God. I stopped and listened but heard nothing else so loud, only some low moaning and bumping sounds.

Being a nosy kid, I slipped back downstairs and tiptoed along the hall toward the activities room. To say the least, I was not prepared for the activities taking place. There was Reverend Broadhead and Mrs. Weston, the choir director, thrashing around on the couch at the end of the room. In short, the ideal of ministerial piety took a big hit in my book that night, which is why I take with a grain of salt most moral exhortations issued from the pulpit.

That memory is probably the reason Earl Anthony started at ground zero with me and only went lower. I don't know any details of his amorous adventures and frankly don't even want to imagine them. However, I do know that when a man of the cloth drives a Bentley, flies a Citation X jet, and works in his own twenty-story building, certain Christian principles have in all likelihood been trampled upon.

In spite of the many faults I find in the man, I couldn't criticize his energy and ambition. Earl was self-made in the truest sense. He'd been raised in a small town about twenty miles southeast of Macon, Georgia. His father, a traveling Bible salesman who never developed the proper affinity for his product, left the family when Earl was seven. His mother raised Earl and his two sisters alone. She was not a pretty woman, Reba Anthony, but she was a determined one.

She worked at two jobs daily for all of Earl's first eighteen years and was adamant that he and his sisters get the best education possible. Reba was better educated than many of the women in Wallace, Georgia, but that meant only that she had two years at a women's junior college. Still, she had acquired an appreciation for what an education could mean in the changing twentieth century.

She was also a deeply religious woman. The children all grew up as members of a strong Baptist congregation. As a boy, Earl probably had a medicine chest full of psychological problems related to his father's abandonment of him, but back in the thirties, people just assumed that everybody had problems, so get over it.

The Anthonys were a hard-working family. They minded their own business and were good citizens, but they were nowhere near the upper echelon of Wallace society, such as it was. Indeed, the very proper congregation of Grace Memorial Baptist church, the Wallace equivalent of Riverview Baptist in Warren where Wiley was a life-long member, looked somewhat askance at the small, country congregation of Mills Ridge Baptist, the one to which Reba and her children belonged. This attitude did not go unnoticed by the young Earl.

Earl Anthony was one of a kind, a unique force of nature. He knew from an early age that he wanted to be a preacher, and he also knew that he didn't want to be a small-time, Baptist, fried-chicken-on-Sunday preacher. Earl wanted to be in the big time, a Billy-Sunday type. A lot of folks today probably never heard of Billy Sunday, but in the first quarter of the twentieth century, he was the biggest thing around. To want to be that big was to want a lot.

Earl's ambition knew no bounds. As a young man, he was always serious about his studies; always conscientious about his jobs; always loyal in his church attendance; and always firm in his belief that someday the whole congregation at Grace Memorial could kiss his ass.

One of the many similarities between Earl and Wiley was their determination to "show 'em;" except Earl had more than a vague notion of who " 'em" was. He had taken down names and addresses.

By the late fifties, Earl Anthony had become the Reverend Earl Anthony. He had gotten his undergraduate degree from Bob Jones University, Betsy Graham's alma mater, and his divinity degree from The New Orleans Baptist Theological Seminary, a fundamentalist institution located in a green but unfashionable part of the city.

While there, Earl made the acquaintance of the Reverend Lamar Bloomfield, executive director of The Center for Christian Action. CCA was a kind of evangelical think tank, funded primarily by a man named J. Rex Hunter. J. Rex had made his fortune in the "awl biddnes" in Texas and Louisiana, and was politically to the right of Caligula. He funded the center as a personal atonement. Word had it that Rex had not always been a fellow who toed a rigid Christian line.

Because of Earl's energy and driving ambition, the Reverend

Bloomfield offered him a job with CCA upon graduating from seminary. The organization had announced, several months before hiring Earl, a major research program to quantify the contributions made to American family values by the evangelical movement. Earl was hired to work on this project.

It became clear to anyone with a teaspoon full of intelligence that what CCA and Rev. Bloomfield were really doing was compiling a national list of evangelical Christians, especially those with big check books. This list, segmented on a regional basis, starting with cities, then counties, states, and eventually geographic regions of the country, could be a veritable gold mine for CCA. They, of course, denied any intention of financially benefitting from this information.

In addition to the general ledger containing millions of names, a high-priority list of top evangelical leaders was also prepared. This one received special attention. The end-game of this effort was obviously to control the largest list of evangelical Christian names in the country. Such a list, updated on a regular basis, would prove to be invaluable to conservative politicians and leaders of the evangelical movement.

For CCA to benefit financially from this information would prove to be tricky, since any "for-profit" use of their assets could jeopardize their tax-exempt status. If, however, a list of names was "given" to certain CCA friendly individuals contemplating a run for political office, then who could object—other than the opposing candidate?

It worked like this: Contributor A makes a tax-free contribution to CCA. CCA, after a discreet amount of time, furnishes a list of its donor names, correlated by location, to Candidate Y to help in his campaign. The fact that Contributor A might likely be a supporter of Candidate Y's issues would, of course, be irrelevant. Within CCA, this research program was known as ACE, short for American Center for Evangelism.

As happened frequently in Earl's charmed life, he left the organization at just the right time. Six months after he left, Reverend Bloomfield was indicted on several counts of pedophilia and embezzlement. Earl, when questioned by the grand jury, acted as if he had just seen his mother run over by an eighteen-wheeler in front of their house. He shook his head, clasped his hands, almost wept as they asked questions about CCA and Bloomfield. No! He had no idea that the good reverend was attracted to young boys. No! He had never received nor did he ever know that Bloomfield received multi-million-dollar bonuses. It went on and on, but in the end Earl was exonerated.

It is interesting that within a year of leaving CCA, Earl founded his own ministry, The Christian Crusade, with what appeared to be a national pre-vetted list of names and contact information. Within weeks of financing his new building, he had an FCC license for his broadcast efforts.

But he needed a partner who knew more about media and broadcasting than he did, so he approached WLJC in Atlanta with a proposal for a Sunday-morning program called "The Hour of Salvation." Earl had gotten to know the station's owner, Percy Calhoun, at an industry conference that CCA had hosted and had stayed in touch. He knew that Percy was looking for ways to differentiate himself from the rest of the local stations, and he hoped that his idea for a family religious program might fill the bill. WLJC was not the local market leader, and its Sunday morning schedule was definitely not a revenue golden goose, so the right idea in a weak time slot might have a chance. It couldn't hurt.

In June of 1965 Percy Calhoun aired the first of what would be thousands of broadcasts of "The Hour of Salvation," and the Reverend Earl Anthony was on his way up. The show featured a format for the whole family: great music, stories for the kids, inspirational speakers sandwiched in between Earl's sermons, and a philosophy that called for social and political activism.

By 1980 the "Hour of Salvation" was the most popular religious show on television and by 1990 Earl had acquired his own satellite feed called "The Family Network". Earl dubbed it "The Funtime Channel." Percy Calhoun had learned what all of Earl's partners eventually learned; once you're no longer useful, you're toast. According to Earl, loyalty was okay if you were a Boy Scout but not if you were an entrepreneur.

Earl Anthony had founded an empire based on religion, and while not the first or the only such endeavor, his was certainly one of the most powerful and influential of the era. When Wiley mentioned his idea of using the Christian Crusade as a stalking horse [my words not his], I knew he was right. The crusade was enormous. No one knew how many members it had but the Nielson ratings for the Funtime Channel were huge.

Having Earl on our side would create a lot of PR, a lot of free PR. Wiley wanted me to get a copy of the schedule for the upcoming crusade in New Orleans as well as some idea of where Earl's head was these days. Earl could either be in one of his Sermon-on-the-Mount periods or one of his Warren Buffett periods, and we needed to know which before we confronted him and his handlers. I decided to call Felix Cooper, Earl's director of operations and his longest-serving and most loyal disciple.

⌢

"Felix! William Walpole Bowater the Third here. How are you?"

I could hear Felix laugh on the other end, but then this was not difficult since he had one of the truly distinctive laughs on the planet. Ruth Lee could have heard him if I had held the phone out. It was a noise like no other naturally occurring sound. The best way I can describe it is to tell you to imagine an elephant trumpeting while his testicles are being crushed by a python. It starts somewhere in the contralto range and ends with a lyric soprano fillip, like a DQ curl.

"William, lad, so nice to hear from you. I assume that we shall have the pleasure of your company in New Orleans?"

"Absolutely, Felix, that's what I'm calling about. The senator wants me to brief him on the weekend. Who's going to be there? Who's speaking when? What do you want him to do, if anything?"

"Billy, to save time, let me send you a complete schedule. It will have everyone of consequence who will be there, yourself included, with full biographies. It will list the times and locations for all activities, and last but not least it will give some suggested times and locations for the senator to speak if he is so inclined. And, please remind Wiley that he is staying in the Delta suite right next to Earl on the top floor. I wish I could say the same for you but, alas, you have a deluxe room on the floor below. However, you do have a river view and a balcony. Anything else?"

"No, not really. I'd be glad to help out if needed. Perhaps you have an attractive young woman who is attending the crusade for the first time and is concerned about being alone in New Orleans. Most of my work for Wiley is already done and so I could perhaps escort said young woman around and show her the sights. Allaying any fears she may have about being in such a big sinful city alone?"

Felix again launched his arpeggioed laugh, as I pulled the phone away from my ear just in time to avoid the finish. "I bet you would like to help. That's just what I'd be afraid of, Billy, that you would allay her —and her fears. Thanks, but I got that scenario covered myself."

"Come on, Felix, you know you're too old for allaying anyone's fears." Felix chortled and mumbled something about never betting against his manhood, especially in New Orleans.

I loved the fact that the crusade was always in New Orleans and not Charlotte or Atlanta or some other more wholesome Southern city. In fact, I once suggested Miami as a site for the crusade and Felix just harrumphed and said something like, "Miami, why the hell would we go there? Miami is full of Eduardos and Chiquitas; it's Havana with a parking problem. We're about the South and everybody knows that Florida ain't really the South. Florida is where God put all the Yankees he had left over after making New Jersey. He didn't have anywhere up North to put 'em so he made Florida and stuck it on Georgia's ass."

The truth of the matter is that Felix and Earl love Louisiana and New Orleans. In fact, I've heard from some of my more adventuresome friends that Felix is into some pretty kinky stuff, and that his nights in New Orleans are not exactly filled with hosannas and thank you, Jesuses.

For the Reverend Anthony it's different. Earl has had a familial relationship with Louisiana ever since his days at the New Orleans Baptist seminary. As part of their studies, he and his fellow students at the seminary would sally forth into the wilds of the Louisiana countryside carrying the "Word" to the bedraggled inhabitants of the disparate parishes. Earl got to know the internal organs of Louisiana better than his own. There was even the occasionally whispered rumor that somewhere in the Delta was a child with a surprising likeness to the good reverend Anthony. This has never been confirmed as far as I know, but still there's something that keeps bringing Earl back to New Orleans and the parishes of Louisiana other than preaching the word of God to the un-saved heathens of the Delta.

Felix has no attachment to the countryside. It's the city that holds his interest. There is something about New Orleans, something pre-verbal and atavistic that pulls at Felix. He knows he shouldn't love it, the French Quarter, the cavernous bars and old-time speakeasies along Bourbon Street, the gluttony, the blowsy, baroque cross-dressers arrayed in groups of four or five on the wrought-iron balconies above his head, but he does. The real New Orleans keeps its own company, and only the deepest and most anonymous soul within each of us is welcome there. Crusader Felix stays at the Hilton, but after-hours Creole Felix walks the streets and back alleys of New Orleans looking for companions among Los Caprichos, à Perdu—the lost.

The crusade was set and the invitations sent. Wiley and I would be actors in the play, or at least Wiley would be, while I moved the scenery around and made sure the curtain came up at the right time. There would be things to do and people to see, but also time late at night for me and my secret sharer to walk about and breathe in the sweet and pungent scents of New Orleans.

9.

We got to town on Thursday afternoon, and since the main activities didn't start until Friday, only a small covey of reporters was in the lobby when we arrived at the New Orleans Hilton.

The hotel manager was, as expected, on hand to greet Wiley. Wearing an unctuous grin, he stood bobbing and weaving in the humid afternoon sun. His name was Arceneaux, Norwood Arceneaux. A man of medium height, he was bathed in nervous perspiration and appeared ready, if called upon, to prostrate himself at Wiley's feet.

"Senator, it is indeed a great honor to have you and Mrs. Hoots as our guests for the weekend. If there is anything that you might want, sir, please do not hesitate to call on me personally."

Wiley grinned and saluted the gawkers and celebrity hounds standing outside, then said to Evvie, " Why don't you let Mr. Arceneaux take you up to the suite, dear."

Wiley loved coming into the lobby of a hotel and having reporters rush up with microphones held out to him and camera lights glaring. Today he smiled and waved to the clusters of curious tourists who were whispering and pointing like gossips. As he stood in the lobby of the Hilton, Wiley held up his hand. The waters of the Mississippi didn't part but the crowd quieted.

"Ladies and gentlemen, I'm just a guest at the crusade. My very dear friend Reverend Anthony was kind enough to invite me again this year to his meaningful and uplifting celebration, and again I could not resist the temptation of a weekend of fellowship and inspiration. Washington is mighty short on inspiration these days, but I don't want to turn this into a political show. This is a weekend to unite in praising God, and I for one am going to keep it that way."

Wiley smiled and headed toward the elevators, whispering out of the corner of his mouth, "They're all yours, Billy."

Hardly all mine, but still, mine for a while. Standing there, before the crowd of reporters and curious onlookers, bathed in the camera's lights, it wasn't hard to understand the addiction to all of this...to the throngs of obsequious hangers-on, moneyed lobbyists, and clamoring media types. It's heroin without the needle, more expensive to sustain but eventually as fatal.

A good friend and mentor and an influential lobbyist once told me, "Billy, if I know you want another term in congress, I own you."

"John, that being the case, what's the answer?" I asked him.

"Term limits, otherwise you're asking the junkies to stop on their own and they'll never do that. They cannot, Billy."

⌣⌢

"Senator Bowater, uhm, I mean, Mr. Bowater, Colin Matthews, *Washington Post.*"

"Well, thank you for the passing credit, Colin. A little premature, but appreciated nonetheless. Now, what's your question?" I smiled, practiced my contemplative pause, and danced under the spots for another fifteen minutes.

⌣⌢

The phone rang at seven-thirty the following morning. I was brushing my teeth but figured it was Wiley, so picked up in the bathroom.

"Umhuh."

"Billy?"

I spit and answered again, "Yes, sir."

"Earl wants to meet for breakfast in his suite in fifteen minutes. He's gonna have Felix there and I want you to be there as well. Bring our stuff." Not a request.

"Okay, I'll be there."

I knocked on the massive double doors, then stood back leaving the senator standing alone. Almost immediately the right hand door, firmly in the grip of the Reverend Earl Anthony, messiah of the airways, flew open. Standing there in the entry way to the massive suite with a broad smile on his face, Earl said, "Senator Hoots, my friend, I'm so glad you're here. I'm sorry we didn't have a chance to talk last night, but Felix and I were going over last-minute changes to the agendas. How 'bout breakfast?" As he moved into the living room with Wiley, he looked back and waved me in as well. The Reverend Anthony was in a splendid mood, thank God.

"Good morning, Earl," Wiley replied, "It's great to be here."

Earl guided Wiley to the balcony beyond the parlor.

"I've got coffee, fruit, and biscuits set up on the balcony. We can eat and talk there. William, you come along as well. You know Felix Cooper, I believe?" Felix smiled and winked at me.

"Yes sir, Felix and I have had many interesting conversations."

Earl and Wiley stood against the railing and looked out over the brown, meandering waters of the Mississippi—waters whose calm, sun-dappled surface belied the stream of toxic effluvia running fast beneath the surface, the ejaculate of ten dozen chemical plants between New Orleans and Baton Rouge. Earl started the conversation.

"It's so good to see you, Senator. How have you been?"

"I've been fine, Earl, just fine. Sometimes I think I'm getting too old for this job, but then something happens, and I realize I simply can't quit. Anyway, how are you? That's the important thing on this, the eve of another grand and sacred weekend."

Earl couldn't have been more animated. He explained the spiritual themes of the weekend, who was coming, and what had been happening at the crusade. Wiley would smile and add some anecdote from Washington to which they would both either laugh or offer a short tsk-tsk. After a few minutes, as they looked out over the vast expanse of water flowing below the hotel, their conversation became quieter, more inward and finally, stopped altogether.

Regardless of whether one's perspective is spiritual awe or secular fascination, the Mississippi and her swirling mythology is seductive beyond analysis. The churning, brown water casts a spell over travelers, and as they gaze out over the alternately calm and busy river, they are held immobile until the shrill horn of a barge or tug rouses them from dreams of Tom and Huck and Jim and all their own fantasies of youth and escape. At least for this traveler, these were the fantasies that I imagined. I was always Huck Finn in my early days. Independent, self-sufficient, and courageous enough to be unique.

Earl Anthony and Wiley Hoots stood watching the ships and barges traversing the deceptive currents of the river, until a grain barge sounded an ear-shattering horn to let everyone know it was on its way downriver. The two turned from the river and smiled, dreams dispelled.

The crusaders would be arriving at nine, so Wiley and Earl sat down to breakfast. Felix and I sat at the other side of the table and passed the time with gossip and banalities while Earl and Wiley discussed the state of the nation. Earl had been making a point about what he saw as a crisis in the values of the average American when Wiley stopped responding, sitting quietly with his hands folded in his lap.

"What's the matter? Something wrong?" Earl said.

Wiley smiled. "Not at all, Earl. I was just thinking about what you were saying and how that applies to the election coming up."

Earl leaned back from the table.

"And, how's it going?"

"Earl, I need some advice. My staff and I have been debating media strategy for this year's campaign. As you know, my opponent this year is a very popular man, a man who brings a lot of money to the game. It's the general consensus, at least between Billy and Hoover Leggett, my campaign chairman, that we should play the statesman, start with a warm personal approach. But at Carter & Horton there's the feeling that we need to pursue a more controversial tone; something to put Governor James on the defensive.

"For example, Billy doesn't feel that topics like partial-birth abortion, which Mr. James has supported, should be used so early in the campaign. He and Hoover feel we should lead off with talk about Warren, small-town values, and honesty in government. John Carter, on the other hand, wants to turn it up a notch. He and Willis want to inflame the base with pictures of partial abortions. They want to go for the most sensitive parts early. I'm torn. What do you think?"

Earl sat for a moment then rubbed his hand over his mouth. "I think this isn't my specialty, Senator. Both subjects need to be talked about, just like lots of wrong-headed things the Democrats stand for. You know my feeling about the plight of families in this country—their lost values, misplaced loyalties, retreat from Christian principles. Anyway, I'm sure your staff knows more about this kind of thing than me, but I know that these things must be talked about at some point. We can't sweep our problems under the rug and still hope to save our nation!"

Wiley nodded sagely. "You're so right. But my question is how best to get these topics out. What is the best vehicle?"

"Well, that's one of the great things about the crusade. We bring these kinds of problems before the country. I like to think that this is one of our greatest services."

Wiley turned to me and held out his hand. I handed him the Xer's catalogue as we had rehearsed. He turned to Earl and presented him with the catalogue. Earl looked at it and then back at Wiley.

"What's this?"

"This," said Wiley solemnly, "is the product of a liberal government. This is the cancer devouring the spirit of this country...eating at the morality of the family that you so eloquently describe. This is one of the most heinous examples of liberal secular propaganda that I have seen in the last twenty years. This is the perfect example of a world that has lost touch with God! A world where secular humanists at the universities are trying to put man on the Throne, not Jesus."

Earl scrutinized the cover then looked back at Wiley.

"Go ahead, open it. Look at what your and my tax dollars are paying for."

When he'd reviewed the catalogue, Earl put it down and looked up, raising his eyebrows.

"Isn't it amazing what passes for art these days . . . what passes for education and culture? I just can't believe. . . ." His voice faded out and he sat looking at the open catalogue, shaking his head.

"You see what I mean," Wiley said. "You think I'm overreacting?"

"Wiley, unfortunately this kind of trash is everywhere. Broadcast television is about as bad." Earl cocked his head to the side. "You thinking of using this in your campaign?"

Wiley paused. He'd expected Earl to be a bit quicker on the uptake. "Could be. I know that most people would find this a waste of their tax money, but, Earl, what do you think the crusaders would think of this show? How do you think *you* could use this? I'm really here to help you. How many things do you send out to unite the crusaders to your cause?"

Earl pursed his lips. Before he could answer, Wiley continued. "What do you think the value of a government-sponsored art show done by deviates is worth to your fundraisers? What better example of the loss of family values? How better to get our message out to the country. We can be partners in this thing, Earl. We can join forces to rip this deadly tumor out of our society."

Earl focused on Wiley's face, especially his mouth. After a few minutes, he nodded slightly and then motioned to Felix to take the book.

"You're right, of course, this should not go unanswered. Felix and I will need to discuss this with our staff, but I think this art show might be a very tangible example of our loss of direction in this country. What do you think, Felix?" Felix looked at the picture of "Jordan's Water" that I had pointed out to him and nodded. "Might very well be the kind of thing that puts the problem into the proper perspective. We'll need to get a little deeper into the background of this matter, but this could be valuable," Earl concluded.

Wiley smiled. "I knew you'd appreciate this opportunity, my friend."

I've been to national political conventions, mega sports events like the ACC basketball tournament, even a Super Bowl, but nothing can match for emotion and crazed participants the bi-annual crusade put on by Earl Anthony and the Christian Crusaders. Given the fact that Wiley was a special guest of the crusade, we had the best seats possible in the New Orleans Superdome. I was on the front row, dead center, right where the Saints goalposts would be. All of the broadcast media was behind me with their cameras set up on a platform. There had to be a dozen groups there; everybody from the networks, NBC, CBS and ABC to CNN and the Funtime Channel, which of course had the best spot. All this not counting the dozens of print groups present.

It was almost seven o'clock and everywhere you looked were masses of crusaders. They were laughing, singing, hugging old friends, and in all ways enjoying the fellowship of sixty thousand fellow believers. The keynote speaker for this year's crusade was none other than Dan Hawke, vice president of the United States. While not the brightest bulb in the Washington chandelier, Hawke could deliver the kind of bone-jarring rhetoric that would work the crowd into a lather.

You could feel the excitement. The hall reverberated with the anticipation of pending salvation. Red, white, and blue banners trumpeting passages of scripture hung from the ceiling and covered the walls. Huge crusader shields emblazoned with blood-red crosses wrapped every pillar and post while thousands of colored balloons awaited release from the huge nets suspended above the quivering mass below. American flags were everywhere. It resembled a national political convention more than a religious meeting, and to a large degree it was, except the candidate was never in doubt. Earl Anthony was president for life.

At seven-thirty, the house lights dimmed and the orchestra began its fanfare. Spotlights methodically crisscrossed the hall, and the dizzying tumult that had moments before filled every corner, faded to a reverent murmur. All eyes were on the darkened podium. From the darkness, a single white spotlight, small and focused, began to illuminate the microphones and huge crusader shield that hung down from the lectern. A deeper quiet spread out from that still center and subdued any lingering murmurs.

I held up my fist and focused through my tunnel of fingers on the lectern and the shadowy figure beyond. As I watched, the robed figure slowly emerged from the shadows. The figure became, when touched by the brilliant white fire of the expanding spotlight, the Reverend Earl Caldwell Anthony, founder of the Christian Crusade and self-proclaimed prophet of American values.

Earl glided toward the microphones. When he arrived at the center of the podium, he grasped its sides as if to steady himself, and in a single dramatic motion, ran his hands through his thick white hair then skyward, arms spread wide, palms raised.

"Brothers and sisters—God is with us in this place." The roar was deafening. Every soul in the hall leapt to its feet and yelled, "God is with us! God is with us!"

The spirit had descended upon Earl Anthony, and his voice boomed out over the crowd like buttered thunder. "Jesus is with us in this place!" Sixty thousand throats agreed, "Jesus is with us! Jesus is with us!"

The moaning mass of crusaders raised their arms in the air and swayed from left to right, right to left, responding to Earl's exhortations. They showered the podium with amens and thank-you-Jesuses. I could feel the vibrations of a floor shaken by 120,000 thousand stomping feet and I trembled with it.

⌒

I've never been a man of absolute faith…at least faith as dictated by biblical inerrancy. I have come to believe that there is a plan, that a logical unified field dictates the motion of the universe and life as we understand it, and don't, and that there is a power or being who has set this plan in motion. Such a belief is obviously not something I got from my Sunday School lessons; rather it was the egg-heads and "pointy-headed liberals" in Chapel Hill that moved me in this direction.

Earl and most of the other TV preachers might say that I am faithless because I haven't been born again. That if I will just put my trust in God, he will anoint me with his grace and give me a rebirth. I've never really understood the whole born-again thing. It's not that I wouldn't enjoy unconditional faith, I just don't know how to take my mind out of the process. I keep running into questions that need answers but the only answers the church gives are "because the Bible says so."

Maybe tonight. Maybe, I thought, if I raise my arms with the rest, if I sway and moan and praise the Lord, maybe it will come tonight. Maybe He will come. It has happened before. It happened to Paul. He was an unbeliever and God spoke to him on the road to Damascus. Why not the road to New Orleans?

I looked around to see who was near me and who might be watching. The camera guys were too busy focusing in on Earl and the mass of crusaders on the main floor. The rest of the staff was nowhere to be seen and Wiley was sitting on the back of the stage.

I took one more look around then raised my arms and closed my eyes, a living antenna searching for a signal from God. I swayed back and forth and shouted into the huge canopy of the Dome. I cried, "Thank you, Jesus. Thank you, Jesus!" and made a noise that for a moment came out like Felix's manic laughter. Disordered and almost obscene that I should be acting this way, I figured, "Billy, you're at the dance, so dance away."

I kept my arms raised and my eyes closed, barking out shouts of praise and uttering sounds like those I make while eating a deliciously rare cheeseburger. Eventually, I stopped swaying and shouting and making cheeseburger sounds. I opened my eyes, lowered my arms, and gazed out across the massive domed expanse and its teeming throng of believers. The Reverend Anthony stood wailing from his perch high above the shield and cross.

Okay, no signals received from on high, no salvation tonight...no epiphany, no burning bush, no scales dropping from my eyes. I was still the result of a biological birth thirty-five years ago. I could see the circus clearly, and remember thinking, Billy, look around you. Look at these people shouting and moaning. This is America and America is afraid. Americans fear the way ahead. They fear each other and even themselves—all the uncertainties of the twentieth and twenty-first centuries. Lines have blurred; absolutes have become maybes; truths, hypotheses. A void looms; a vacuum screams, desiring to be filled.

Reverend Anthony stood before the mass of crusaders, arms raised and jaw set against Satan. He promised he would help them... give answers to their questions, solutions for their problems, and an enemy on whom to focus their frustrations and fears.

Zealotry was loose on the hustings and that ole time religion, the warriors of Judges and Samuel, drowned out the truths of the Man from Bethlehem. Love was a crumb for the weak. Earl fairly trembled, electric with revelation, his voice grew stronger and louder.

"God has the answers, my friends. Listen to me. God has the answers, and I—I am commanded to share them with you."

I couldn't help but smile. "Amen, Earl, amen."

10.

"Folks, we're now at our cruising altitude of thirty-eight thousand feet and if you look out the port side windows you can see the city of Baton Rouge. We expect a smooth flight to Washington today. Welcome aboard."

I looked out and down at the city below...Baton Rouge, "red stick," capital of Louisiana. Where the hell did " red stick" come from? It didn't look as big as I thought it should, but then Louisiana isn't really that big a state. More people than Mississippi, but that's not saying a lot. I don't even know what the biggest city in Mississippi is...maybe Jackson, or Gulfport. Whatever it is, there's no city even close to the size and quality of New Orleans. To me, New Orleans is the most unique city in America, and without it, Louisiana is just Mississippi with a French accent.

Based on the numbers, the past weekend had been very successful. Felix said they had raised more money and recruited more new members than at any previous crusade, and that's saying a lot. He also said they had shown the Xers' catalogue to a few of their select members and that almost all had agreed that this was a theme that would sell. He figured that "The Xers' show was just one big sinners' jamboree."

I wonder if Hypocrisy was ever in the running when the church was putting together its list of the seven deadly sins: Pride, Envy, Gluttony, Lechery, Avarice, Wrath, and Sloth, both spiritual and daily. That's my sin, Hypocrisy, with a dollop of Envy thrown in, but of course Hypocrisy is really a good part of all seven.

There I was sitting with the senator and his wife at thirty-eight thousand feet, drinking Blue Mountain coffee, reading the paper, and leaning back in butter-soft leather seats aboard Earl's fifteen-million-dollar Citation jet. What a hypocrite! Maybe we should combine envy and hypocrisy into Envocrisy; that would really hit me on the head.

Billy Bowater, you are guilty of Envocrisy! You indulge yourself aboard a private jet that you constantly criticize but use whenever it's offered and all the while wish that it was yours and not Earl's. Love the sin and hate the sinner, that's your motto.

Wiley waved for me to come up to the front of the cabin where he was reading at a small fold-out table.

"Yes, sir. What's up?" I said, sitting down across from him.

"Billy, I've been thinking about that art show thing and how we can use it. Earl and Felix seem to be really warming up to the idea of publishing some of those pictures in their newsletter, a picture being worth a thousand words, and all that. We need to not only have our own strategy for registering our outrage at the proper time, but to orchestrate Earl's and the crusade's schedule as well.

"I don't want them to prematurely publish those pictures until we are properly organized to react. We need to have a meeting with Carter & Horton and Hoover as soon after the Fourth as we can. Evvie and I are going to be in Raleigh for the Fourth. I'm speaking at the fairground after the parade. In the meantime, I want you to have the staff research the show, the artists, reviews of the show, the university personnel involved, and anything else we should know about. I don't want to step on my Johnson on this one."

I watched Wiley as he talked and saw that if I had ever wanted to downplay this thing, that possibility was gone for good. Earl and Felix would never forget about this show even if we did. In fact, they would obsess about it until they convinced themselves that it was their idea in the first place. A result that wasn't altogether unattractive.

The crusade was always on the lookout for programs that could create outrage among its followers. Outrage equaled money and money was air time, jet fuel, more crusades and more power . . . power to shape national policy . . . power to expand Earl's empire. For the crusade, deliciously obscene and sacrilegious paintings and photographs in a federally sponsored art show could be the fundraising equivalent of a blind child in leg braces petting a rescued three-legged dog on the Jerry Lewis telethon.

I must have looked concerned or perhaps agitated because when he finished telling me what to do, Wiley said, "So, Billy, what's the problem? You look unhappy." Unhappy was okay. I just didn't want to look confused because that would mean I wasn't in control. I never wanted to give Wiley that impression.

"No, sir. I'm not unhappy but I am concerned. I recall we talked about this before we went to New Orleans. I don't want to anger a lot of our friends from Chapel Hill. You know much better than I the number of your supporters who are die-hard Carolina fans. While the university clearly has a liberal reputation, many of its graduates are right-thinking, conservative supporters of ours, and we need 'em to be happy with us."

Wiley smiled, but it wasn't a something's funny smile or a smile borne of a past memory. It wasn't a cat-swallowing-the-canary smile, either. It was a pull-the-wings-off-the-canary smile.

"Billy, I realize that you have your loyalty to Chapel Hill. I can understand how as a Morehead you'd be sympathetic to the school, just like I understand how so many graduates of that place never get over having gone there. But in this instance, I don't give a damn, plus where else but me are they gonna go?

"I've swallowed so much Tar Heel crap over the years that my craw is stuffed. I realize that an art show at a university museum isn't the end of the world, but whether you agree or not, the fact that taxpayers' money is used to support some perverted bastard's idea of art is quite possibly symptomatic of the problems in this country. Maybe this Pope fellow is just trying to impress a bunch of arrogant academics but if so, that's just as serious. Why does such trash impress a bunch of educated adults? That's the question.

"I'll tell you why. Because they know it aggravates conservatives, and they know that people like me and Earl and millions of other ordinary, hard-working folks resent having our tax money spent on such bilious crap. They enjoy spitting in the face of good Christians.

"Billy, you understand what we're doing. Even if you don't believe in a lot of it, you understand why I feel the way I do. I don't care if you agree. I don't care if you support my beliefs. It would be nice to have an AA that was sympathetic, but that's not why I hired you and it's not why you're still here. You're here to be my CIA, my Secret Service, my secretary of commerce, and my accountant. Oh, yes—you need to be my assassin on occasion as well." He paused.

"Billy, I didn't hire you for your morals, quite the contrary. When my staff said you'd had a small scrape with the state bar, and when I checked around about you, I knew one thing for sure and found out two. What I knew for sure was that the son of William Bowater Jr. was a man of consequence. That your scrape with the state bar was probably a put-up by someone who was trying to get back at your father for some perceived slight or even some decision made as attorney general.

"The two new things I learned about you are: first, you're as smart as they say you are. Second, you'll do whatever it takes to get the job done. If it ever gets so you can't do what needs doing, let me know and I'll write you a glowing letter of recommendation." Never taking his eyes off my face, he leaned back in the soft leather seat.

If he was trying to see what I was thinking, I didn't let my eyes speak. Silent impassivity was my protection. It allowed Wiley to assume whatever he wanted. I could be whatever he wanted by nodding slightly and looking contemplative.

Wiley was right about my loyalty to Carolina. I owed the place a lot—a great education, clever and loyal friends, a worldly perspective he never got at his Baptist school, personal pride, hubris, and a belief in

myself, or at least an understanding of myself. Chapel Hill gave me —
me. It added a foot note to the Bowater & Bass expectations script that
there was more to life than those ghosts. It raised the curtain on the
unique possibilities for the life of William Walpole Bowater the Third.
But the part about not hiring me for my morals hurt. My scrape
with the state bar ethics committee, an organization that is hardly a
lighthouse for moral navigation, had to do with a misunderstanding
about solicitation of business within the medical establishment. I did
nothing wrong. I was cleared. And for the ethics committee of the
profession to throw stones at its members for their methods of business solicitation is the height of hypocrisy. The legal profession spends
more money on television, newspaper, and yellow-pages advertising
than do the automobile dealers of America. I have little patience with
such hypocrisy—I prefer my own sin, envocrisy.

But Wiley was right about what he hired me to do. My job was to
allow him to bathe in his moralizations and self-delusion while I did
the dirty work. As noted, when called on, I arrange the bouts and take
the punches. To quote Don Corleone, the character on whom all other
red-blooded American men have a man-crush: "It's not personal, it's
just business."

11.

"Ruth Lee, would you please get John Carter on the phone?"

"Just a minute, Mr. Bowater."

It wasn't a good morning. Wiley was on a tear and it had spread throughout the office. Ruth Lee, not much fun on a good day, had lapsed into her prickly-bitch mood; however, within a few minutes I heard her say, "Good morning, I am calling for Mr. Bowater from Senator Hoots's office. Is Mr. Carter available for his call?" I'm guessing that the receptionist at Carter & Horton had then called John's assistant who in turn called John. Then, John being John, he probably asked his assistant who was calling. She undoubtedly said that it was me, or rather my office, thus, John was waiting a sufficient number of screw-you-Billy minutes before answering. I looked at my watch to see how many screw-you minutes I rated this morning. Four minutes, a little less than usual, meant he wanted to talk. It really was an infantile game we played.

"Billy, what's up?" John Carter's voice boomed out of my speaker phone. I jumped slightly then turned down the volume.

"Well, at the moment I'm waiting for my ears to stop ringing."

"Huh?"

"Never mind, John. Listen, I want to confirm the timing for this Xers thing. Wiley wants to meet sometime this week or early next week to discuss a strategy." John said nothing.

"John, you still there?"

"Yeah, I'm here. You're talking about that art show thing, right?"

"Yeah."

"I don't really know all that much about it and obviously don't know what you two are thinking." And then with his usual pout he said, "You know, nobody has kept me or Willis in the loop on this thing."

"That's probably my fault, John. This was something that Wiley's daughter wrote to him about and that he asked me to investigate. I met with the folks in Chapel Hill who put on the art show and then reported to Wiley. I really didn't think it was anything of great substance, but he took a copy of the catalogue to New Orleans and showed it to Earl Anthony and Felix Cooper from the Christian Crusade. Long story short, they like the idea of using some of the pictures from the show as a theme for their next fundraising effort, so Wiley wants to see how we might segue our ads into their campaign.

"You know, make this look like Wiley is jumping on board the train that they started instead of the other way around. I told him of my concern about unnecessarily pissing off our Carolina funding base, but you know how he feels about Chapel Hill."

John laughed, "Let me guess. Would something like, 'fuck them', pretty well sum it up?"

"Yeah, that's about it."

John gave a low hummmm, then said, "Okay, let's try for Monday morning the eleventh at about ten. In the meantime could you send over a catalogue of the show plus any other material that will help educate us? I'll call later today to schedule a short conversation between yourself and Willis and me, okay?"

I hung up with a guttural grunt meant to pass for 'yes' or 'okay' or whatever, but without actually saying anything. And yes, I was being as childish as John, but then John always brought out the puerile in me.

⌒

Carter & Horton was housed in an elegant suite of offices located a block north and west of the National Gallery, average for Washington but pretentious by North Carolina standards. Wiley and I showed up at nine-fifty, ten minutes early. The receptionist, after genuflecting before Wiley, rushed into the offices behind the high-ceilinged waiting room to find John and Willis. Wiley sat down in a large wing chair and started reading a recent copy of *National Rifleman*. I chose *The American Spectator*.

I looked at my watch, five after ten. Here is one of John Carter's key clients sitting in a reception room waiting for his paid consultant. The arrogance was incalculable. Wiley put down the magazine and slowly looked around the room, taking in the half-dozen or so English hunting scenes and the mass of miniature floral prints geometrically arranged on the mocha-colored walls.

"What light-in-the-loafers decorator you think did this place?" Wiley said under his breath. "I bet this job paid for his sex change operation."

I smiled, "I don't know about the sex change operation, Senator, but whoever did this job was well compensated."

"Who's the guy in the portrait at the end of the room?" Wiley asked.

I looked at the huge painting. " Got me, but he looks like he died of acute constipation."

John Carter opened the door and came into the waiting area. "Senator, I'm terribly sorry but I was tied up on a phone call with one of your fellow legislators about a matter of immediate and grave importance. Please forgive me."

Wiley mumbled something as he walked past John and into the boardroom. I hoped fervently it was "Screw you, John," but I doubted so.

The Carter & Horton boardroom ratcheted up the pretense of the reception area. A conference table the size of an aircraft carrier dominated the windowless room, and more bad hunting prints lined the walls. At the far end of the room were a half-dozen three-foot foam-core boards covered with colored bar-charts and ragged trend lines. A projection screen hung from a giant crevasse in the ceiling.

Willis pointed to two seats at the end of the great table. "Gentlemen, please." Wiley sat at the head of the table and I sat to his right. John and Willis sat down, John next to Wiley and Willis next to me. Probably some strategy lay behind this arrangement, but I couldn't quite see it or really care to think about it.

"Senator, how can we help?" John said, all smiles.

"I assume you have reviewed the catalogue that Billy sent over. The one on that so-called art show at Chapel Hill?"

"We have, sir." John replied.

"I also assume that you have considered the possibilities of us partnering with Earl Anthony and the Christian Crusade to publicize this matter?"

"We have some ideas along those lines," John replied with a sneer.

"Based on your somewhat emotional plea for a crowd-pleasing horse to ride this summer, I think Billy and I have arranged your ride." Wiley looked at me and smiled, then nodded toward John.

"Mr. Bowater, why don't you illuminate the subject," Wiley said.

I briefly recounted my conversations with the staff of the Ackland, my conversations with UNC's Carl Fanceler, our trip to New Orleans, and our subsequent conversations with Earl and Felix, and finally our internal research which more or less confirmed everything that Evan Lee and Ginna Humphreys had told me. Willis took a few notes while John closed his eyes and affected his sage Dalai Lama mode. After I finished, I turned toward Wiley with an inquiring look and slightly raised hand.

Wiley shook his head and looked at John, who had by now opened his eyes and was looking pensively toward the ceiling.

"Senator, I think this is the *perfect* horse. Exactly the kind of thing that can get the blood pumping and the wallets open." He looked down from the ceiling and directly at Wiley. "You and your daughter have discovered campaign gold . . . full marks."

Full marks? What an asshole. John Carter heard someone on the BBC make that comment during an interview, so he incorporated it into his repertoire. It lives there with his other Anglo-isms, words like bloody good, the loo, and fortnight. In his mind, using such words made him appear more pandemic; however, in the words of my favorite Anglophile, Oscar Wilde, "Illusion is the first of all pleasures."

King John continued. "Senator, Willis and I have discussed this situation and feel that a federally funded art show that glorifies deviate lifestyles is the perfect vehicle to demonstrate how far this country has wandered from traditional American family values. We have already started to outline a theme, timing for that theme, and a schedule tied into Reverend Anthony's exposure of this show. I was on the phone with Felix Cooper this morning and we are scheduling a meeting to sort it out."

I looked at Wiley then held up my hand. "John, aren't we getting a little ahead of ourselves? I mean, we haven't even talked to Felix about what they might want to do. Who told you to call them?"

John turned his kiss-ass smile away from Wiley and shot me a very sincere fuck-you glare. "I wasn't aware that I needed your permission to call anybody, Billy."

So many biting insults and put-downs crowded my mind, but remembering my promise to Wiley, I counted to twenty not ten.

"Excuse me, Mr. Carter. Let me rephrase that. Why, when this is the first discussion we've had about whether this material is even relevant to the campaign, are we calling the Christian Crusade in order to hammer out details? I believe the senator has the final word on our strategy, unless, of course, you feel that you don't need his approval." Wiley cleared his throat and stepped in to end the hostility.

"Okay, gentlemen. Enough of this. I believe that we do need to have a consensus on this material, John, before we go charging off and spending money on something that will not net us very much. And, Billy, if John gets good intel from the crusade, then we're that much better off, are we not?"

The conversation improved from there. Within thirty minutes we had decided that we would indeed create a new series of ads which featured "the crusade's discovery" of this blasphemous show. But not until the end did I realize what John really had in mind.

"So, John, you guys are going to write something that highlights this show based on the 'discovery' of its contents by the Christian Crusade and then blame Governor James and the Democrats. Oh, and in particular the National Endowment for the Arts, a pet agency of the Democrats, which supports this kind of depraved exhibition. Good so far?"

John rubbed his chin, pushing his lower lip up. "More or less. Strategically, I believe we need to highlight actual pictures and artists. Maybe say something about the disgraceful practice of rewarding and publicizing deviates for their misguided attempts at art. We should briefly show small elements of certain photos and paintings with the caveat that showing the whole work would not be appropriate for family consumption. The truth is that most people will imagine stuff that's a whole lot worse than the actual pictures. We can say something like 'Exhibiting such filth is against everything that America stands for.' I haven't written anything yet, but you get my drift."

I did get his drift and didn't like the direction one bit. I nodded and said, "Yeah, I understand what you're getting at, but don't you think that attacking two individuals who had nothing to do with the show except getting nominated and awarded is a bit unfair. I mean, let's go after the NEA and its policies, not some poor schmucks who had nothing to do with selecting or curating the show."

John looked at Wiley, who made no attempt at replying, and said in his sonorous, patronizing way, "Billy, people don't know who the NEA is. It has no face. It doesn't paint or photograph homoerotic pictures. It doesn't stand for deviate personal behavior. It's not a person, and we're talking to people. We need human faces, human smut, human sin!

"These artists are symbols of the deviate lifestyles that the Christian Crusade and Senator Wiley Grace Hoots have been working to expose. Their 'art' is at the core of the problem. They are the disease that is spreading through our society. What . . . "

I couldn't stand it anymore. "That is such a crock of shit, John. These two were nominated based on the quality of their work. They weren't selected as poster children for homosexuality. You don't even know if they are homosexual and even if they were, that's nobody's business. Shit, Leonardo da Vinci was homosexual. You ever heard anybody trash his work because he was gay?" Wiley stood up. He was looking at me with something less than approval. I took a deep breath and tried to look calm, tried to count higher than ten, tried to be a fellow who got full marks.

"William, no one is saying that we need mention the names of these two people, though the name Christian Pope does anger me greatly. We are saying that some of the works in this art show celebrate the homosexual lifestyle which a Christian nation does not condone. We are saying that continuing to ignore this assault on our beliefs and the beliefs of most Christian families has got to stop. The federal government has got to stop spending our money on this trash.

"And by the way, if you think that painting a picture of our Lord tongue-kissing John the Baptist or a photograph of naked little girls hugging under a waterfall does not pretty well establish the sexuality of these so-called artists, then you and I are further apart than I thought." Wiley was getting angry. He mouth was becoming stiff and grayish, and his lips tight and narrow. I needed to stop the bile.

"Senator, I don't know anymore than you or John what the sexuality of these two artists is. What I am saying is that attacking individuals who had nothing to do with creating this show can backfire on us. It can make people feel sympathy for the artists. Make people feel like we are attacking innocent bystanders."

Wiley rolled his eyes. "I believe I just said that we aren't going to mention them by name. We don't need to say squat about these two deviates, but we need to show their work and point out that it, the work, celebrates a deviant and blasphemous lifestyle. If people get their names, that's not our problem. We can always put it on the press. Besides, having some queer Amos painter lionized by the press won't hurt us."

Wiley used the term "Amos" whenever he was referring to blacks. He had used "nigger" for most of his adult life but after getting to the senate, he was advised that using that term would mean disaster, even if used in private conversation. The safest rule in Washington was to treat no conversation as private, because eventually somebody would say to the press that they had heard Wiley use the "N" word in conversation, even a private one.

I didn't want to fight anymore. I would modify the strategy if I could, but mainly would try and keep the heat on the federal government and its participation away from Chapel Hill and the two artists. I made a mental note to learn as much as I could about both Christian Pope and Aeriel Sopwith so that, if possible, I could portray them in a more sympathetic light. I didn't recall much information about either artist, but then most catalogues are vague on an artist's personal history, especially ones featuring young artists. I needed to call Dr. Humphreys and also get Ann Murphy to have our press clippings firm do a search in the local papers around Asheville and D.C.

Wiley stood up and shook hands with John and Willis, then headed back to the lobby and the elevator. Willis followed Wiley and then John, who stopped outside the room and waited for me. As I passed him, he put out his hand and said in his most sarcastic, pseudo-Anglophile voice, "Carry on, William. Stiff upper lip."

I smiled and shook his hand, hoping that it brought to mind either a day-old flounder or, better yet, a wet diaper.

12.

I was delayed getting out of National, which meant that I got to Raleigh later than planned, but then the last time anyone got out of Washington on time, it was on horseback and the rider's name was Washington. I called Lucy when I landed at Raleigh-Durham but she didn't pick up. I left a message that said I was going to the hotel and that if she was free to meet me there for dinner.

I added that she would enjoy the menu special for tonight . . . crow and Bowater sashimi. I knew she'd want to chow down on me for all the ruckus raised by the crusade and now the Hoots campaign over the Xers show. She had already started last night when I called her.

"Luce, I'm coming to Raleigh tomorrow and thought that we could . . . "

"Could nothing, you asshole." Not the opening that I had expected.

"What the hell is eating you?"

"Oh, I don't know. How 'bout an article in the *Washington Post* titled, 'Earl Anthony crucifies Carolina art exhibit.' You read that one?"

"Yes, and I read the article in the *Times*. Look, Lucy, if you're pissed at not getting the scoop, then fine, but believe me when I tell you that I was as surprised as you were. No one in Earl's organization told us they were releasing their barrage this week. If I had known, I would have given you a heads-up. I'm sorry, but we didn't know."

"Right."

"Look, what's done is done. I said I'm sorry."

"Okay, okay. But, Billy, when you told me about this show a few weeks ago, you said it was no big deal. You said it was a bunch of young artists spreading their wings. Now I find out that somebody wants to clip their wings and spoil their Ackland nest. What the fuck is going on and what the hell does your boss and his asshole buddy Earl think that they can get out of this? It's a college art show, for Christ's sake! Who gives a damn?"

"Come on, Lucy, you know better than that. For the senator this is an issue of where and how to spend public money. The crusade sees itself as the defender of family values. I might think it's bullshit, and you certainly do, but most of evangelical America doesn't. You know the drill."

She did know the drill, but was in no mood to acquiesce. I told her I would call when I got to Raleigh but hung up believing that it would be a pointless call. I had tried to explain what I was dealing with but to no avail.

All my warnings about offending our Carolina donors had fallen on deaf ears. Wiley had listened to John and all I could do was try to keep the most offensive parts of the campaign ads aimed toward the NEA rather than at the artists and the university. I knew I had only so much power in this regard, but I could try. The campaign, I told myself, would be better off with me still in a senior position than without me, so my only choice was to modulate my words and actions. I hoped this was true and that I had discovered a strategy which would let me sleep with a soothed conscience, but as we all know, it's hard to convincingly lie to your own mind, even when it tells you to try. So try as I may, I couldn't find the pleasure in this illusion.

"I like my job," I once told Lucy, "But that doesn't always mean I love my job." This was especially true today. Still, being an AA in

Washington beat the hell out of most of the other things I'd done. At least I was in the action and not soliciting malpractice suits in Warren.

After checking in at the hotel but still not hearing from Lucy, I went downstairs with the idea of having a few drinks and something light from the menu. When I walked into the bar, there, at a tall table covered with appetizers and drinks, sat Lucy Sue Tribble, scourge of the powerful. I smiled and shook my head.

"How the hell . . . ?" She cut me off.

"How, nimrod? When I saw that you called and then found out when your plane landed, I called Claude, my main man for deep intel at the Velvet Cloak, and told him to order for us since you were on your way and I was coming over. I wanted to surprise you."

"Well you certainly did." I leaned over and gave her a warm kiss. "Thank you. This is a great ending to a rather shitty day." I sat down opposite Lucy and took a long slow pull on the single malt she had ordered for me.

"How 'bout one of those Camels, Miss Surprise-a-Minute?"

Lucy smiled and shook out a Camel Light, holding the lighter at the ready.

"So what was so shitty today?"

I inhaled deeply, waiting for the nicotine to do its numbing thing. "Well, let's see. First, I had a meeting with John 'the Baptist' Carter about our strategy for the next few weeks. I'm trying to move the campaign emphasis from homosexual art to the S&L financial crisis, education, and defense spending. John wants to milk the Xers art show until its tits are dry, plus get on board with Earl and Felix in bashing homosexual lifestyles and the evils of abortion. It's the 'We're getting the shit kicked out of us on the real issues so let's dig up some irrelevant bullshit to shovel' strategy. I keep saying, John, we're the incumbent. We don't need to act crazy . . . enough with the homosexual agenda, but it's like I'm speaking Urdu for all the attention I'm getting."

"By the way, Lucy, what the hell is the homosexual agenda other than trying to get laid in a different way? I mean what do Earl and Felix think these folks want? Pink tights and toe shoes for the football team?

Crew cuts for all the girls in the homecoming court? What a bunch of bullshit. Who the hell would bother recruiting little rednecks to the bliss of homosexuality, anyway? None of my gay friends. I mean, what are they thinking?"

Lucy was smiling. "What makes you think I have the slightest clue what those two assholes are thinking? And don't act so naive. You know what they're up to . . . money and power, just like your boss."

"Well, at least you didn't lob me into their scrum this time."

"Only because I don't want to fight with you tonight."

Lucy had a way of getting quickly to the quick. She knew I wouldn't want to talk about the Xers ads and thus she moved the conversation to more neutral territory. However, she couldn't leave the arena without at least throwing a few punches.

"There is the question still before us, Counselor, of how long you can stand being part of an organization that does shit you don't condone."

I waited a few beats before framing what was a risky reply, given that I really wanted to get laid that night.

"I guess," I said, "about as long as you can stand being a member of an organization that pries into people's private lives while hiding behind the disgraced excuse of the public's right-to-know; publishes hearsay as the truth on a regular basis; harasses people who you know are probably innocent in order to titillate your readers' basest desires; and regularly slanders people and institutions that your owners don't like, all the while wrapping yourselves in a banner with 'FIRST AMENDMENT: FREEDOM OF THE PRESS' blazoned across its face."

Silence. We sat there nibbling on cheese and crackers, taking small swigs of our drinks, and deciding what to do next.

I decided first. "Okay, truce. We can both eviscerate the other's employer, so let's not. Let me, since we are on the subject, tell you what I can about the Xers situation." Lucy leaned back with a reasonably entertained expression.

"Please do," she said.

I took a piece of paper out of my pocket. "After that truly bullshit press conference and press release by Earl and the Crusade, we had a meeting at Carter & Horton where we discussed what if anything we would use from their release since the die had been cast and you surely realize that Wiley had to respond. John said he felt we should quote liberally from their piece, but I advised that since it was written from an entirely evangelical Christian point of view, we should be more secular and unemotional. I won round one.

"On the next issue, I didn't do so well, but I did win points. When the campaign released its first reaction to the crusade's opening salvo, the language was toned down considerably from the original piece and yours truly was the reason." Lucy didn't react, so I moved on. "The original statement prepared by John Carter included the following . . . 'This use of federal and state tax dollars to assist a small group of sexual deviates in trumpeting their immoral lifestyles, etc.' But, if you recall the piece you were given, Lucy, you will remember the following: 'the use of federal and state tax dollars for an art exhibition that questioned traditional moral standards and gave voice to individuals who document what are to many people unhealthy and immoral values . . . ' See what I mean?"

Lucy finished her martini, leaned forward, and looked up from the table.

"So that's it? That's what you feel is a significant change. Come on, Billy. That's just window dressing. The same implications are made. The same points are gotten across. The . . . "

"Stop. Words matter. Definitions matter. Of all people, you should know that how you say something can be interpreted many ways and if people want to see the dirt they can. Censors are the dirtiest people around. They see smut in everything, even when it isn't there. They're looking for dirt, so they always find it. I changed the language in order to not smear Pope and Sopwith, the two artists. If people make assumptions, then so be it, I can't help that. At least I didn't let them be called 'sexual deviates who are trumpeting their immoral lifestyles.'" Lucy nodded.

"I'll give you that, Billy, but you know that's not gonna keep them from being called up and questioned. As a matter of fact, after your and your buddy's little bombs in the papers, yours truly has been given the job of writing a feature story on this whole thing for the *Observer*, which means interviewing the museum personnel as well as the artists, judges, and NEA people. It will also mean interviewing the Christian Crusade, Wiley, you, John Carter, and anybody else involved. You up for that?"

I finished my scotch and waved at the waitress. "Hon, how about another Macallans and another martini for the lady."

Lucy looked at the waitress. "Remember, very dirty and lots of olives."

I took deep breath and let it out through my nose. She was gonna do the story whether I was up for it or not. "Lucy, you got a job to do just like I have. You do what you gotta do, but be fair."

"Same for you, Billy. Be fair...to me, to Carolina, to the artists. Don't do something you'll be ashamed of."

"Like I said. I don't call the shots, and, by the way, neither do you. When your editor tells you to add something to your article that you don't feel is needed or relevant, and you don't do it, then you can criticize me and I'll believe it." Lucy didn't look too pleased.

"What makes you think I've ever juiced up a story based on an editor's directive?"

I leaned back. "Okay, how 'bout the time you wrote that story about an illegitimate kid that some candidate for the state house had had fifteen years before. His opponent admitted that his campaign was the source of the information, but still you guys published the smear without condemning the source. I mean, what the hell does fathering a child fifteen years before have to do with his qualifications to serve in the state house? You just loaded the evangelicals' shotguns for them."

"We didn't lie. We didn't make it up. We reported the fact. That's a lot different from making shit up."

"Like what? Make up what?"

"That the artists in the Xers show are gay. You don't know that."

"Exactly, that's why I took out of the press release that they were sexual deviates. Let's see what your article ends up saying about that."

I was exhausted and getting more tired as we argued. "Lucy, let's drop it. I don't want to think about blasphemy or homoeroticism. Let's talk about something else."

"Like what?"

"I don't know," I put on a big smile. "How 'bout them Heels? We gonna win the ACC this year?" Lucy was so shocked she snorted into her martini, spilling some of it on the canapés as well as her own slacks. She put her glass down and, laughing all the while, wiped off her pants.

"Like either one of us could give a fuck . . . but you're right. Tonight should be for fun."

We both decided that we could think of better things to do than munch on fingerling eggrolls and chicken nuggets, or at least think of a better place to munch on them.

I caught the eye of the young woman behind the bar. "Miss, could we have these to go, and could you send another round of drinks to Room 300?"

13.

You know you've been staying at a hotel too long when the folks at the front desk know the brand of scotch you drink, what you'll want for breakfast based on how you looked the night before, how much starch goes in your shorts, and who you're sleeping with. Based on these criteria, I had been at the Velvet Cloak too long. No way around it, though. I'd be here a week or ten days managing the campaign schedule.

September was less than a month away, and Wiley's campaign was moving into high gear. That meant I was on the road to a normal life. Wiley had pulled ahead in the money race thanks to a team of Raleigh computer gurus that Carter & Horton had hired. More money meant that our campaign ads were appearing more often. Governor James's ads carried the standard anti-Wiley messages highlighting his opposition to *Roe vs. Wade*, his planks on education reform, such as the neighborhood school mandate, his anti-gun control position, his racist history, and his extremism in general.

None of this bothered the senator. In fact, he loved being called a "far-right demagogue." He laughed at the press corps' dubbing him "the radical candidate" and "the darling of the far right." During a luncheon speech, he came up with a line that found a permanent place in the Hoots lexicon: "They're correct about one thing, my friends, I am the most right person in this campaign . . . and Governor James is the most wrong." He loved it, and used it numerous times in the months after.

I managed to curb most of his extreme diatribes, but occasionally one got through during the heat of the moment. A week before, Wiley was speaking to a group of wealthy businessmen in Raleigh, all of whom were contributors to the conservative John Locke Foundation, when he said that a piece of legislation he was proposing was the result of a blasphemous art show in Chapel Hill. His audience knew by then what he was talking about. He ended his speech by asking the assembled crowd for money to help him "Stop liberals from spending taxpayers' money on perverted, deviate art that a bunch of queers think might make them famous!" This brought thunderous applause and whoops from the audience. By design, no members of the press were invited to the luncheon, and given the political leanings of most of the attendees I doubted that anyone would even discuss what was said, much less quote Wiley to anyone in the press.

At one point after Wiley's speech, a gentleman named Art Bishop stood up and yelled, as if he were witnessing in a Pentecostal tent meeting, "Who's with me? We've got to stop the radical left-wing from stealing any more government money, our money! I'm tired of paying for these so-called artists to attack Christianity and human decency. They're using their 'art' to promote immorality and homosexuality. You know it's true, so who's with me?"

It was a sight to behold. I knew some of these men. In fact, I had met Art Bishop a number of times. He and Father were business acquaintances, which is to say that Bowater & Bass had represented Mr. Bishop and his family company in some of their dealings in eastern North Carolina. I had done some work for Bishop & Company while I was working at Bowater & Bass, so to hear Mr. Bishop rail against the artists' lack of human decency, when I knew some of the shit he had done in his business and private life, made me want to laugh.

The John Locke Foundation was and still is sponsored and paid for by several very conservative individuals in North Carolina, Art Bishop among them, in order to spread the gospel of John Locke or what they purport to be the gospel of John Locke. They consider themselves a think tank with a neutral political philosophy. Strange then that they routinely flog "liberals" and "secularists" in the press with the most vituperative and flamboyant language they can muster. John Locke, described in most history books as a liberal social thinker of the seventeenth century, is thus transformed into a British version of John C. Calhoun, the nineteenth-century South Carolina senator who justified slavery based on the Bible.

⌒

Robert, the Velvet Cloak's restaurant manager, smiled when I showed up for breakfast at six-thirty. With order pad in hand, he said, "Got in early last night, didn't go out, up early this morning—means a long day ahead. Egg white omelet, dry toast, two Camels, and a go cup of bold coffee. Am I right?"

I laughed, "That's good enough, Robert. I was dreaming of steak and eggs, but your choice is healthier. Let's pretend the egg whites cancel out the Camels."

"Absolutely, Mr. Bowater."

I had to be in the Raleigh headquarters by seven A.M. since John Carter, Hoover Leggett, Wiley, and I, along with some of our local media gunslingers, had scheduled a one-hour conference call to solidify the senator's schedule and media buys for the final two months. It was, as predicted, turning out to be one of the most, if not *the* most, expensive senate races in the state's history.

While media buys and advertising content were not part of my responsibility as Wiley's AA, a fact that John Carter often pointed out, the senator seemed to enjoy my contributions and usually asked that I participate. I agreed, my main reason being to piss John off.

The truth is I loved it. I enjoyed trying to anticipate and then counter our opponent's moves. It was a game, a chess game, a war without bullets—except the electronic ones fired by television. The governor routinely flayed us for deceiving and lying to the innocent citizens of North Carolina, so we retorted with equally preposterous claims of malfeasance—punch, counter punch. No harm no foul.

For example, on our morning conference call, we approved a new advertisement which accused Governor James of calling for racial quotas. This was, like most of Wiley's ads, total bullshit. Governor James had said that he was looking favorably on a piece of legislation proposed by Senator Kennedy concerning affirmative action. The bill called for employers and school administrators to be "aware" of racial harmony and balance—a rather innocuous bill that simply tried to make racial awareness part of the hiring process. Nothing was ever mentioned about or intended to require a quota; however, John Carter's ad said that employers would be required to hire a certain percentage of minorities. Check.

Governor James has claimed in an ad that Wiley will repeal the law requiring background checks on people who want to buy hand guns, thus allowing dangerous criminals to buy guns. Check mate.

I told Lucy that my job was to manage the senator's schedule and office personnel, not the lies he tells. If she knew that I also worked on some of our ads, like the racial quota ad we just approved, she would skin me.

Wiley loved the ad. In fact, the quota claim took over first place in his speech priorities, moving ahead of the homosexual agenda of the federal government. This didn't mean that he was abandoning the Xers' ads, only that his tried and true favorite, race, had more power as a donation motivator in these last crucial months.

When Lucy started to give me grief about Wiley's tactics and I told her that I didn't write or produce any of the ads, she characterized this as wearing blinders and ear muffs so I could ignore the smoke and screams from the furnaces. As usual, she used the most noxious and ridiculous analogies to describe my job. But, as I often told her, neither she nor anyone else could understand my job, or me for that matter.

How could they? They weren't there every day. They didn't deal with Wiley every day. They hadn't led my life.

Nonetheless, some folks like to imagine themselves as the wise and sage interpreters of other people's motives and actions. I characterize this as employing the "Atticus Finch Platitude." Atticus Finch was the main character in Harper Lee's book *To Kill a Mockingbird*. I won't try and recount the story here, but at one point near the end of the book, Atticus's daughter, Scout, the narrator in the book, is standing on her neighbor's porch—Boo Radley's porch. Boo has always been a mystery to Scout and her brother Jim, so as she stands there on Boo's porch she says to the reader, "Atticus always said that you could never really understand a person until you consider things from his point of view, until you climb into his skin and walk around in it."

I've thought about that piece of advice ever since I read *To Kill a Mockingbird* for the first time, and after all these years, I've come to the conclusion that stripped of all its sweet-as-apple-pie crust, it's just bullshit wrapped with a pretty bow. It can't be done. My skin only fits my body. It can't be stretched or shrunk to fit anyone else—and my shoes, same thing. I know what Atticus meant and it's a noble sentiment, but I also know that it's impossible to truly understand another's soul, no matter how hard you try. You can't recreate their life experiences. You can't relive their embarrassing moments, their traumas, their joys. And you can't understand a life of suffocating expectations if you've never known them.

How do I imagine being a woman? How about a black woman—who's Jewish? Let me imagine what it's like being a black man who is brilliant but turned away from every one of his state's prestigious universities because he is black. The what-ifs are endless, but the absurdity of the premise is not—that's simple. No one can ever know what it's like to be William Walpole Bowater the Third because no one can ever re-create my life! You think not? Okay, live this:

"Are you going to be attorney general some day, William?"

"I'll bet you're proud of your old man. Attorney general for the state of North Carolina, and maybe our best ever."

"You know, William, Bowater & Bass has been so important in this community. It'll be a big job keeping it going and growing, but I know you're up to it."

I have a lot more of these memories, but you get the picture—just not the reality. And it's in reality that real pain and fear live.

I know, enough self pity. That's what my grandfather used to say. That was what he said just after he said to me, "William, if the son doesn't surpass the father, then he's a failure."

Don't put on my skin unless you want a rash or my shoes unless you want blisters.

⌒

The Raleigh campaign headquarters, being at street level, gave me a clear view of the comings and goings in and out of the office. We were situated just off Capital Square, and within sight of the Old Capital Building. It was a great location, available through the generosity of one of Art Bishop's companies. Since Art owned the building, he had the leasee, a travel agency, vacate the space for five months, paying their costs of moving up a floor.

I had opened the slats of the venetian blinds so I saw Lucy striding down the street and into the outer office. Here she was, with a voice that could carry for three counties.

"Excuse me, but where can I find that low-life William Bowater?" Everybody in the office knew who she was. Had it been anybody else they would have been dialing security, but with Lucy it was like stand-up comedy.

I got up and opened my door, and leaned out into the bigger room, "Ms. Tribble. I'm sure we all appreciate your calm, professional demeanor this morning." She looked at me. "I had a fairly good demeanor a few days ago, but then I started listening to some of the people Senator Hoots finds objectionable and lost it. My demeanor is now pretty crappy. On top of that, it's gotta be a hundred degrees outside." I forced a smile and motioned her into my office, shutting the door.

"Goddammit, Lucy, why the hell do you have to pull this shit right in front of the whole office? I guarantee you that one of those nimrods is on the phone to Washington right now. I'm just glad Wiley is at home in Raleigh. Shit." I didn't need this right now. I didn't need Lucy putting me in such an uncomfortable position.

"And I care about that why?"

"Well, maybe because you say that you care about me to some degree, all evidence to the contrary." This was enough to pop her inflated sense of indignation. She bowed her head, then looked up a bit unfocused.

"You're right. I'm sorry, that was uncalled for. I apologize and will do so to the assembled flacks in the outer office."

"No, let it pass. They're used to your . . . exuberance. Quiet humility might frighten them even more." She laughed and then leaned back, looking around.

"You got any coffee in this place?"

"I thought you said that it was a hundred degrees outside. Why do you want coffee?"

"Caffeine fix. You don't allow nicotine indoors, do you?"

"No."

I walked over to the door and looked out. "Susan, would you mind bringing me and Godzilla two cups of coffee, sugar and cream for both? Thank you."

We sipped our coffee and looked at the desktop, out the window, at the coffee but not at each other. Finally I looked up from a memo on my desk and directly at Lucy.

"Okay, Luce, something is bugging you. What gives?"

She didn't say anything for a few more beats. "I've been talking to one of the artists from the Xers' show and you have no idea the toll all this 'queer,' 'deviate,' and 'perverted' language is taking on her. She's in danger, very fragile." I started to respond with something about the usual state of political campaigns, over-zealous advisors, sensationalism in the media, and so on, but Lucy held up her hand.

"Stop. Don't even try to justify this shit. I've heard this all before and I'm telling you that it better stop."

"Lucy, you might as well try and stop elections. This kind of stuff has been going on since the eighteenth century. Christ, this is just the way it is."

Lucy's eyes bored into me. "Yeah, I know, but I'm telling you, Billy, Aeriel Sopwith is on the edge."

"So what am I supposed to do about it? I don't think that calling her and reminding her that this is just politics will win many points. Listen, it's just a fucking game. They call us names, we call them names. They lie about us, we lie about them. It's a game, a huge chess game played out on television, radio, and in the newspapers."

"Chess game my ass, Billy. Maybe to you and Wiley and Governor James it's a game, but not to Aeriel. It's a game when you're the one moving the pieces around the board, but it's not a game to the chess pieces. It's not a game when you're the pawn and some big son-of-a-bitch grabs a knight on a horse and knocks your ass out of the game. You testosterone laden assholes *choose* to play the game. You have the option to play, Aeriel Sopwith and Christian Pope don't. They're carried to the board in a box, put on a square, and forced to play. What I'm telling you is that I don't want Aeriel going home in a box."

I sat there looking into my cup of coffee. Her emotions and anger had sucked the oxygen out of the room, as well as out of me. I waited until I felt the heat subside, then caught my breath.

"How do you know it's that serious?"

Lucy looked at me with her all-too-familiar, "Are-you-fucking-stupid?" look.

"I spent two hours on the phone with her about a week ago and have talked to her at least four times since then. This morning being the most recent. Billy, she is gay but hasn't fully come to grips with it yet. She has a partner, but as far as her mom and dad are concerned, the woman is a roommate. Her folks live in Asheville and she and her roommate live in Greenville. She teaches at East Carolina in the art department. Your friend at the Ackland, Dr. Humphreys, thinks Aeriel is one of the best young photographers in the country. She has won praise from a lot of major institutions."

"Lucy, I'm sure she is good, but again, what the hell am I supposed to do about it?"

Lucy shook her head, "I don't know. See if you can't stop the name-calling. I don't know—but you'll figure it out if you want to."

"The biggest name-callers are Earl and Felix, and I have less than no sway with them. Wiley is really just quoting from their releases, and by the way, I did, as you recall, get the campaign to talk about lifestyles and generalities instead of individuals."

Lucy stood up and opened her steno pad.

"May I quote from a recent article in the *N&O?* '. . . perverted, deviate art that a bunch of queers think might make them famous?' What bunch of queers would that be, Billy? Generalities? Stop jerking off and get serious." She had a point. Wiley believed he could say whatever he wanted about homosexuality because God was on his side. I thought that given the audience, the queers quote would never see the light of day but someone called the *N&O* and gave it to them. Hard to imagine anyone in that room having the balls or moral conviction to take the time to call it in.

"Lucy, you remember a guy named Carson Everhardt who died of AIDS last year?"

"Yes."

"Wiley's comment when he heard that Carson had died was 'He was a homosexual, acknowledged to be. He died of AIDS and I'm sorry about that, but the fact remains that he was using his talent to promote homosexuality.' Carson was a musician and tried to raise money and build awareness of the AIDS epidemic. But Wiley had made up his mind – 'AIDS is strictly a homosexual disease, God's retribution against the ungodly.' Trying to argue him out of that position is as pointless as trying to convert him to Islam."

"So get the hell out, Billy. You don't belong . . . "

"We've been through this a million times. Let's not rehash."

Lucy nodded. "Yeah, yeah. You're not the one elected. You just work for him. Blah, blah, blah. Untouched by human sin."

She put her hand in the air, giving me a jerky wrist wave as she turned to leave but then turned back toward my desk. "Let me ask you something. Just between you and me and the desk there. Does he really believe all the shit he puts out or is he just the best con artist ever produced by North Carolina?"

"I'll tell you a story about Wiley. Close your pad and sit down. Please." She did, but I waited until her smirk was gone.

"I asked Wiley one time about his father. I asked him whether he got his convictions about religion and the world from him. He sat there, maybe deciding whether to trust me, then said that one day he and his dad were walking in the woods at the edge of their farm outside of Warren and Wiley asked where their land ended and where their neighbor's took up. His father nodded and started walking toward a thicket on the other side of a large bean field. When they got there, his father told Wiley to walk over to a big holly tree at the far edge of the thicket.

"'Now,' his father said, 'wrap your arms around the tree.' This seemed curious to the boy, but he did it, turned and wrapped his arms around the tree. With that, the father took his walking stick and slashed it across Wiley's back, leaving a deep, bloody gash and breaking one of the boy's ribs. Bleeding and in shock, Wiley said he turned around and looked at his father, not knowing what to say. The old man's expression never changed.

"'I reckon now, son, that you'll never forget where our boundary is,' the old man said.

"That's how Wiley learned most of his life lessons . . . religion, morals, family duty, God and country. From the holly-tree beating he said he learned how to distinguish right from wrong, what constituted a God-fearing Christian man, and what made a coward. He learned where all the boundaries are.

"Wiley believes in firm, finite boundaries, in a stern, no-nonsense God, one that uses his walking stick to teach. My guess, Lucy, is he believes in that God more than Earl Anthony or Felix Cooper do. Those two are jackals feeding on the scraps that fall off the table of ignorance and fear. But Wiley's driven by something real, something hard." I stopped. How much could I trust Lucy?

"You remember who said just between you, me, and the desk, right?"

"Yeah, I remember."

"And you meant it, right?"

"Yes."

"Wiley set them up to raise hell about this show, Earl and Felix. They would have had no more idea about the Xers' show than flying to the moon if Wiley hadn't shown them the catalogue. John Carter has been pushing us from the beginning to find an issue that can inflame the base . . . the folks that believe in the rod, in boundaries, in simple uncomplicated explanations, ideas easy to understand. What's easier than a dirty or blasphemous picture?

"Lucy, you know as well as I that politics today is all about bumper-sticker-deep ideas. Wiley's comment about queers wasn't supposed to get into the paper. No press was invited and none were there. Someone, and I would love to know who, if you ever find out, called you guys and gave you the quote.

"But I gotta tell you that Wiley isn't sorry it got out there because his folks love it when he says that kind of shit. That Ms. Sopwith is upset is nothing I can help with. I'm sorry, but this is a train that I can't stop."

Lucy sat there, thinking. After a few breaths she said, "Funny thing about that holly tree, nothing else would make sense."

I looked at her, waiting for something else, but she didn't say another word.

"What do you mean?"

"Holly trees are supposed to be sacred somehow. I remember my mom calling them 'holy trees' or 'Christ's thorn' because of the sharp leaves. I guess that's the reason the leaves and berries are used on Christmas. Funny thing, though, the berries are poisonous. I don't remember all the particulars, but I do know that there's a lot of myths —holy and evil—surrounding hollies, so it makes sense that Wiley's boundary tree would be a holly." She stood up, shook her head slightly and said, "You're right when you say you can't stop these maniacs from the track they're on . . . maybe I can do something."

"Like what?"

"One thing about the power of the press, Billy, is that properly directed it can focus a lot of light on plants like nightshade and toadstools that crave darkness. I don't know where the light might shine in this case, but I'm gonna find out." She turned and headed out the door. "I'll call you. I need to have a call with your boss for my article. A face-to-face would be even better." She looked at me over her shoulder.

"I imagine he'll prefer the call, but I could be wrong," I said.

"Okay, I'll be in touch. How long you in town for this time?"

"I'm in Washington tonight and back next week. I'll call you."

"See ya, Billy." Lucy closed the door gently.

14.

The only thing worse than a lobbyist is a cheap lobbyist. I was just back from Raleigh when I got a call from a lawyer representing the North Carolina Coastal Developers Association, a group of white-shoe bubbas who built cheap houses on the Outer Banks. I didn't know this guy very well, his name was Mickey something, but I knew Radar Looper, the head of the contractors Mickey represented, and I couldn't stand him. You could always tell when he was around by the slug trail he left; plus, he made Renn Foster look like a Rhodes Scholar.

Mickey said he was only in town for a day or two and would appreciate a meeting. I hemmed and hawed and whined about being just back in town, swamped with work, and blah, blah, blah. I thought I'd convinced him that a meeting wasn't possible when he implied, in a somewhat oblique way, that a robust monetary figure might be coming our way during the latter stages of the campaign. Enough said, or at least enough implied. I asked him where he was staying and he said Georgetown. Assuming that he was on a budget as obscene as most lobbyists', I suggested we meet at the Four Seasons on M Street for drinks and then go to Odette's for dinner.

Unfortunately, the Coastal Developers were too cheap to give Mickey a reasonable travel allowance; so, after I suggested the Four Seasons and Odette's he said, "I'm staying at the Georgetown Inn on Wisconsin. How about drinks and dinner there?"

Grudgingly, I answered, "Fine, but we have to make it an early evening. I have a lot of work to do before election day."

"Okay," Mickey said, "The Georgetown Inn at six-thirty."

"Fine."

The Georgetown Inn is a block south of O Street in the middle of Georgetown. It would take a while to get there—D.C. afternoon traffic being what it is—so I needed to give myself plenty of time. Besides, a few drinks before meeting Mickey would make the evening less painful. Since I was leaving early, I'd park on O Street and walk down Wisconsin rather than getting bogged down in hotel parking.

I left the office just before five. The traffic from the capital to midtown was moderately heavy, but from there to the Rock Creek Parkway it became surprisingly light. Some down-time would be welcome after the past week.

O Street, being one way, I had to go down to 33rd, turn a few blocks north, then back east toward Wisconsin. O Street was a typical megaexpensive Georgetown residential byway. Most of the houses were old and narrow with little or no space in between. Some were huge with massive grounds, but most were nineteenth-century row houses.

About a block from Wisconsin, I saw a parking spot on my right. There was no sign to the contrary, so I snapped it up. Once on the sidewalk, I looked around at leafy green residential Georgetown. Sublime. The pristine rows of old houses, most of which were undoubtedly redecorated to the Nth degree, stretched as far as I could see in both directions. But I knew Georgetown was far from serene; it was the mastodon of elite neighborhoods. It stood not just for money, but for the power money brings, political power. Beverly Hills was rich and lapdog-pretty; Fifth Avenue was rich and Clydesdale-strong, but

Georgetown was rich, pretty, and strong; strong enough to step on and squash lap dogs and plow horses with nary a thought.

The building where I'd parked was a typical example of the Georgetown motif and had undoubtedly been someone's town house when built. It was now a shop or gallery of some sort. I looked at the sign over the front door: R. Donnovon Art Gallery. R. Donnovon, R. Donnovon, something about that name was familiar. I shook my head and started down the street toward Wisconsin and my appointment with the barman at the Georgetown Inn.

Ten steps later, I stopped. The R. Donnovon Gallery was the first name on the list of exhibitions provided by Mr. Christian Pope of generation X fame. I know this because I read through the damn *Xers* catalogue a least a dozen times looking for language I could use to mitigate the crusade's attacks. When we were flying back from New Orleans, Wiley told me to do some research on the artists, reviewers, jurors and anyone else connected to the *World View of Xers*. I did what he wanted, but along the way, allowed myself the right of editorial review.

No reason to stir the pot for the wizard. He could and would do that without my help. But I did look into the background of the *World View of Xers*, and found what Evan and Ginna told me I'd find—a well planned and executed art exhibit. The only relevant artist information in the catalogue was the artist's city or state, education, and where he or she had been exhibited. Christian Pope was listed as living in Washington, D.C., earning a B.A. in art from American University, and showing in perhaps a half-dozen juried and non-juried exhibits. I remembered that the R. Donnovon Gallery was the first place listed on his page of credentials.

I walked back down the sidewalk to the gallery and up to the front door. I tried the handle but it was locked. I tapped on the window to the right of the door. A man peered around the corner of what must have been an office in the back. Paintings and photographs of every size were stacked against the walls. When he saw me at the window, he walked from the back and slowly opened the door.

"I'm sorry, but the gallery is closed," he said.

"Yes, I see, but I'm only in town for the day and was hoping that I could come in. Are you Mr. Donnovon?"

The man stood expressionless in the open doorway. He was taller than six feet, wearing a Redskins baseball cap, a Bob Marley T-shirt, and a pair of very large wrap-around dark glasses. Imposing in his dignity.

"No. Mr. Donnovon is out of town. Be back Monday."

My curiosity was piqued. "Listen, as I said, I'm in town just for a day, and I really wanted to see if Mr. Donnovon had any painting on display by Mr. Christian Pope. I was in Chapel Hill a few months ago and saw an exhibit at the Ackland that had some of Mr. Pope's paintings and was fascinated by them. Do you know Mr. Pope?" He smiled slightly and nodded.

"Yeah, I know Christian. We were in school together. He uses a studio out back to paint in."

"Really? Is he here, by any chance?" I asked.

"No. He hasn't been around much ever since that Bible-thumper did a job on him. Him and that shit-head Wiley Hoots really have messed his mind up."

I smiled and nodded, hoping to smooth out the man's mood. "Yeah, those pricks have really done it this time. Like I said, I really like Mr. Pope's work and was hoping I could see some more." I stepped into the doorway. "By the way, my name's Bill Walpole." I put out my hand. "I'm a lawyer from Atlanta and have been active in the High Museum down there. I collect contemporary art, and like I said, really fell for Mr. Pope's work." The tall black man softened his expression and took my hand.

"I'm Doc Banner. I live a few doors down and look after the place when Robert is out of town. I also do his books since I'm an accountant. That's what I was doing when you knocked."

"Nice to meet you, Doc. Sorry if I bothered you." I tried to look crestfallen. "Guess you ought to get back to the books, as it were." I turned to go when Doc said, "Mr. Walpole, a minute. Come on in, it's hot out there. A few of Christian's paintings are hanging in the back gallery. I don't know anything about them, but you can look and take notes if you like." I smiled and nodded again.

"Thanks. I'd like that." I walked into the front room and followed Doc to the gallery in the back. I looked at the paintings leaning against the walls—very impressive, too. When we got to the back gallery, Doc turned on the overhead spots and pointed to the wall on my right. There, hanging in a line were three paintings by Christian Pope. Two were portraits and the third was a street scene. It was a picture of three people sitting on a park bench. They looked to be hungry and one to be stoned. The bench was on the edge of some kind of green space, a small park perhaps, but not one to which you might take your child.

"There's a kind of desperation in his work." I said to Doc. "A darkness that seems to defy the possibility of light. One is both drawn in and repulsed at the same time. That man on the end of the bench looks like his soul is already dead."

Doc didn't say anything, just stood against the far wall with his arms crossed. I turned and looked at him and said, "I don't mean to pry, but why does he only paint desperation? What kind of person is he?"

Doc pushed away from the wall but with his arms still folded. "He's the kind of person who keeps to himself. He's the kind of person who paints instead of talking or writing. I've known him for five or six years and I can't tell you ten things about him."

I smiled, "Well, then tell me nine."

It was his turn to smile. "Maybe eight. Christian was raised in D.C., and what I do know is it wasn't no easy raisin's. He has a momma but I never heard him talk about a father. He carries a horn in his gut about a lot of things, mainly about being poor and black at the same time. Being black in D.C. ain't no bed of roses, Mr. Walpole, but being poor and black is the shits. Christian paints to get out. We all—those of us who got gut horns—do something to get out. I studied numbers. Christian studied colors and light."

I watched him speak and tried not to appear smug or uninterested. But I wanted to know about the deviate thing. I wanted to know if Christian was homosexual. I was trying to think of a way to get there without making Doc mad or turning off the slight conversation we had going.

"Doc, what has been his reaction to the things that Reverend Anthony has been saying about him?"

Doc paused a few beats then said, "He doesn't give a shit. They're gonna say whatever they want. He can't fight 'em. I bet there ain't a day goes by over the past few months that somebody don't call here to ask questions about Christian. Robert basically tells 'em to go to hell. He says that it ain't anybody's business how a man or woman lives. But I'll tell you this, Mr. Walpole, people who misjudge Christian Pope make a big mistake. He ain't no still-water puddle. You step in his shit be ready for a raging torrent."

I smiled. "Well, thank you, Doc. I won't take up any more of your time. I appreciate you showing me these paintings. I'll call Robert when he's back. You got a card or something with his numbers?" Doc nodded and walked back to the office and came out with a business card. I took it as we walked back to the front door, shook and said good-bye. The tall black man, Doc, looked at me through those impenetrable glasses and said, "Take care Bill, and tell 'em down there in Atlanta that a Christian Pope is on the way; they better get ready." He smiled, wryly, then closed the door.

15.

I thought the interview went well. I'd been nervous about Lucy Sue doing the Xers' article in the first place, but even more so after her comments on the power of the press to shine lights on what it considered to be the dark spots in the news.

Wiley had reluctantly agreed to a phone interview with Lucy. Originally he had wanted to meet her in person, but John Carter—and for once he and I agreed—felt that in person Wiley might give away too much. If nothing else, his expressions might both provoke and answer too many questions.

We scheduled the call for the first half of September while we were in North Carolina. I was back in Raleigh after a ten-day stint in the Washington office. Lucy was none too happy with our schedule since it pushed her up against her publishing date, but she didn't really have a choice. Wiley was her primary source after all. I suggested to Wiley that we could combine a campaign swing with a short vacation before the final dash in late September and October. Fortunately, he agreed.

We spent the first three days in Raleigh, then a day in Warren for photo ops, finishing up with two days of speeches in Wilson, Rocky

Mount, and Tarboro. I had hoped to see Mother and Father while we were in Warren, but they were in Florida. Though not wanting to seem too mercenary, I asked them, since they wouldn't be using it, if Lucy and I could stay at their place at Pawley's Island for a few days of vacation. They said it would be fine.

The senator's conversation with Lucy had lasted about thirty minutes. He took the call in his study at home in Raleigh, a comfortable, frumpy room with a fireplace and lots of overstuffed furniture. Once during his interview, Lucy had asked Wiley about art in general, something like "Do you ever go to a museum to see art, or have you ever bought any art?" Wiley had smiled at me and pointed to a painting hanging on his wall.

"As a matter of fact, young lady, I am sitting here with Mr. William Bowater looking at a favorite painting of mine given to me by the famous North Carolina artist Mr. Robert Timberlake. It is of an old man, sitting at a table, with the Bible open in front of him and his hands folded in prayer. It is the most inspiring thing to me. In fact, we have ten or twelve pictures of art, all of which I like. But you know, we don't have a single one of homosexuals kissing or of naked girls embracing."

When the interview was over, Wiley looked at me. He didn't say anything at first and I remember thinking he looked like an overstuffed jowly frog ready to strike out at a hapless fly.

"You still seeing that woman, Billy?"

"Yes, sir, I am on occasion."

"Be real careful what you say to her, son. I don't need to tell you how dangerous a person like that can be to this campaign. In fact, I would prefer that you didn't see her during the rest of the campaign just in case something slips out while you two are—" he looked at the ceiling, "—in an intimate situation."

I gave him a non-committal gesture, tight lips moved upward, a slight nod of my head and eye brows that shrugged. No way was I going to stop seeing Lucy when I was in Raleigh. No way that even Wiley was gonna tell me who I could and couldn't see.

"I'm always careful, Senator."

He looked at me with what I call his snake-to-the-mouse gaze. A look designed to freeze you with fear of pending digestion.

In any case, the interview went well. Wiley remained calm, no doubt a major disappointment to Lucy Sue. He hurled no oaths into the face of secular humanism, issued no detached ramblings on the country's abandonment of God. No, the senator had hewed close to John Carter's warning and kept his cool. He was beginning to realize he had an issue that came with its own fireworks, and that public sentiment would force the game. John Carter sensed that the press was starting to smell a populist issue brewing, so all Wiley needed to do was to cloak himself in relatively silent self-righteousness and act the discouraged and worn-down patriot.

"I have tried," he said near the end of Lucy's interview, "for all these years to warn the citizens of this great country about the dangers of a government bent on dictating humanistic morals to us, but the 'intellectuals,' the 'mightier-than-thou's' always said we were crying wolf. Well, Governor James, how do you like them teeth? How do you like that howl?" Wiley ended his interview with a pledge to make sure that "This kind of scurrilous waste of the taxpayer's money will no longer be tolerated."

Lucy, per her promise to me to be non-provocative, obediently took down Wiley's comments with a minimum amount of sarcasm. She was careful not to reveal anything I had told her about Wiley giving Earl the catalogue. My fear was not that Lucy would forget anything, rather it was that she would lose her temper and blurt out something she shouldn't. Thus, I kept some of the juicier tidbits to myself as a matter of self-preservation on the sure knowledge that if she really knew everything, she might explode. She had started researching her article two weeks ago and Wiley's was her last interview. The only person on her list that she had not spoken to in person was Christian Pope, a real frustration since he was the artist she most wanted to talk to.

Dr. Richard White, the chancellor at Carolina, decided to speak on behalf of the university and the museum; thus, the members of the art department had declined interviews, in deference to Dr. White. That and the fact that Evan Lee had said that they'd better not open their mouths to anyone from the press. According to a brief conversation I'd had with Evan, Dr. White was none too pleased when he discovered the amount of information the museum and I had exchanged.

Ginna was told to call the artists and jurors involved with the Xers' show to alert them to the heightened controversy. She reminded the Carolina faculty about making no statements on behalf of the university, and she asked all of the outside participants to answer questions with regard only to their personal involvement and feelings. Some of the jurors, in particular, were outraged at the attempt to discredit the NEA, and they said so.

Aeriel Sopwith was visiting her mother and father in Asheville when Lucy got hold of her for their phone interview, but Aeriel wouldn't discuss the show or the controversy in front of her parents. After a rather traumatic encounter with her father, though, Aeriel called Lucy back and unloaded her frustrations.

Christian Pope was a different story. He was not listed in the Washington phone book, so Lucy Sue contacted what she assumed was a gallery familiar with Christian's work, the Donnovon Gallery on O Street in Georgetown, the first one listed on Christian's exhibit credentials page. When she told me about her phone call with Mr. Donnovon, I didn't mention that I had been there. Some things are better left unsaid.

In any case, her call hadn't made her very happy. Mr. Donnovon gave her precious little information about either himself or Mr. Christian Pope. Other than the fact that Christian lived and worked in a studio behind his gallery, Mr. Donnovon was pretty non-committal. He did say that Christian had spoken with the people from the Ackland a few days before and had been alerted to the probability that someone from the press would call. He said that Christian had asked him to tell whoever called that he did not wish to be interrogated about his work; in his opinion, the press does not want the truth, only the most salacious gossip possible. Robert said, quoting Christian exactly, "What the press really wants is to start a war of words between Messrs. Anthony, Hoots, and myself, but a war of words is playing on their turf, not on mine."

Lucy tried to assure Mr. Donnovon that she was only interested in the facts surrounding the exhibit and that personal information was not her primary interest; however, she said that some biographical information could be important to her readers since a good life story was always valuable in deciding where one's sympathies lay. Christian's opinions about the Xers' show would also be helpful in explaining the motivations and priorities of the artists selected. Clearly her argument fell on deaf ears. Neither Robert Donnovon nor Christian Pope was interested in explaining "their story." Regarding the question of sexual preference, she didn't even hint at that. She said she closed her call with a plea for more biographical information on Mr. Pope, and again got nowhere. Robert did say he would mention it to Christian, but to not hold her breath, unless, of course, she liked holding her breath and then to feel free to do so. The humor was lost on her.

To say that Lucy was annoyed with Messrs. Pope and Donnovon would be like saying that Franklin Roosevelt was annoyed over Yamamoto's Sunday visit to Pearl Harbor in 1941.

Until I was sitting on the porch of Mother and Father's house at Pawley's Island, drinking a rum something-or-other that Lucy had made, I hadn't realized just how tired I was. I needed some time away. I needed to be with Lucy.

She and I sat for hours watching the gulls and pelicans gliding down the beach and listening to the waves breaking on the sand. We walked in the early morning tide, picking up shells and pieces of interesting flotsam that had washed up on the beach. We ate copious quantities of shrimp and soft shell crab, drank rum, and made love in a room with windows opened on three sides, thus letting the moist salt air cool our quiescent sweaty bodies.

For the first two days not a word of politics or office chatter passed between us. We hadn't taken a pledge in this regard, rather it simply never occurred to either of us to start a conversation that had any possibility of ending with a disagreement. We didn't expect such bliss to last for the whole five days, and sure enough on the third day Lucy got a call from Aeriel Sopwith. We were sitting on the porch.

"Hello?" I said, picking up the portable phone.

"Is Ms. Tribble there?"

"Who's calling, please?"

"This is Aeriel Sopwith in Greenville, North Carolina."

"Just a minute, I'll see if she can take the call." I looked over at Lucy and mouthed "Aeriel Sopwith." Lucy motioned for the phone.

"Hello, this is Lucy."

Out of respect for her right to say whatever she wanted, including dumping on me, Wiley, and the crusade gang, I patted Lucy on the head and walked down to the beach for a stroll.

16.

When I got back from my walk, Lucy Sue was still sitting on the porch looking out at the ocean. I didn't say anything, just sat down and waited for what I knew she would tell me about her conversation with Aeriel. Without looking at me, Lucy started speaking to the ocean.

"I never told you about my conversation with Aeriel following her visit home, did I?"

"No."

"After I spoke with your boss, I got hold of Aeriel in Asheville. She was visiting her folks. Thought she might tell them about her and Fiona. She couldn't talk when I called because she was just working herself up to it; however, she called me back the next day. She was back in Greenville. It seems that before she could begin the conversation, her father, having read the press releases from the Christian Crusade and the replies from your office, had a verbal meltdown. To quote Aeriel, 'Lucy, he just exploded. He called me a queer, a sinner, a dweller of Sodom. He said that he could never hold his head up in Asheville again, that everyone would believe him to be a failure as a father.'

"She left the house without ever saying a word about her and Fiona."

She didn't tell them how much Fiona meant to her, how wonderful she was, how pleasant their life together. She just left—the despised daughter of a self-righteous, evil man."

Lucy sat for a moment and gathered herself. Her voice had begun to crack and her eyes were red. I started to get up and move over to her, but she motioned for me to sit back down.

"In our conversation today, Aeriel informed me that her partner, Fiona, is considering leaving her, or at least getting away from what has become an intolerable situation. She and Fiona have been together for several years, and the girls Aeriel frequently photographs are Fiona's nieces…two adorable children that Fiona often takes care of. She loves these children and often keeps them because it's helpful to her sister who is single and travels for her job.

"Fiona's sister, Erin, is upset about the negative publicity over her daughters' being photographed naked, though it's not like she never knew that Aeriel was taking their pictures. In fact, she was proud of the recognition they got from the galleries and publishers who represented Aeriel. I guess when Wiley and Earl started calling Aeriel a queer and implying pedophilia, it became a little too much for her, because she has said that until further notice the girls can't stay with Fiona and Aeriel.

"Fiona feels that she may have to move out in order to see her nieces." Lucy slowly turned to me. "Still proud of the campaign strategy?"

I took a deep breath. "I never told you I was proud of the strategy, Lucy. You know that. If you want to beat me up, Wiley and Earl being far away, then fine, but I can't see that that will make you feel better."

She nodded. "You're right. It won't make me feel better and you're also right that you never said you were proud of the strategy, but let me go on so you can understand what's happening that you didn't plan for."

"I realize that the 'queer' quote, one of Wiley's heartfelt rants, was not one that the campaign gave to the press, but I also know that since it got out there, no one has rushed to deny it or apologize for it. The Christian Crusade, an interesting misnomer since there is nothing Christian about those bastards, has mailed out over five hundred thousand leaflets asking the sheep in their flock to write letters to their congresspersons objecting to spending taxpayer money on 'perverted, deviant art.' I assume that it's only a matter of time before Saint Wiley does the same sort of mailing to his supporters.

"The upshot of all this busy work for Christ is that Aeriel has been bombarded with hate mail, obscene phone calls, and the cancellation of a future exhibit by her employer, East Carolina. Fortunately, there is a bit of sunshine in this dreary forecast, her main gallery has stuck by her and as a show of support, many of the faculty at East Carolina are forming a protest against the university.

"Another pleasant surprise, in an otherwise shitty story, has been the support she has gotten from her fellow traveler, Christian Pope. Clearly she has had a lot better luck speaking with him than I have . . . not surprising really. She met him at the opening of the show in Chapel Hill and while they had a pleasant conversation, she didn't feel they'd made any lasting connection. But it turns out that she made a closer connection than first thought. He has called her on several occasions to offer support."

"What kind of support." I said.

"Encouragement, anger, revenge, humor . . . you name it. It seems that Christian is taking this a lot better than Aeriel and is trying to help her see what he feels can be a positive side. He says there is nothing they can do to stop the Reverend or Wiley from screaming into the night, but that in the long run it might work to their advantage. She finally did laugh a bit when she recounted one thing he said. She said, 'Lucy, do you remember what Oscar Wilde said?' I said I didn't. 'He said that the only thing worse than being talked about is not being talked about. Do you think that's true?' I laughed and said it could be. I tried to be positive. I tried to smile through the phone and lighten her load. But no matter what I said, there was always a flip side, a person with a dark word or phrase that would bring her down.

"Oh, and here's the chief downer—her father, that fine Christian who drove her from her childhood home, is no longer speaking to her. Her mother is apparently more understanding, but Daddy has decided that in order to maintain his upstanding position in the local Baptist church, he must condemn, in public, the lifestyle of his only daughter. Apparently his pastor is a devoted follower of Reverend Anthony and a member of the crusade. He has made sure to supply Mr. Sopwith with all the pamphlets and mailings about Aeriel from the crusade.

"So, what is Aeriel's current status? I would guess, based on our conversation, that she is on the brink of a nervous breakdown." Lucy stopped and sipped from her drink.

I looked over at her and then back at the sea. There was nothing to say. Lucy was right. I should be outraged; I should march into Wiley's office on Monday and resign amid accusations of destructive un-Christian behavior, but what then? Run back to Warren? Get a job with one of the K Street lobbying factories in Washington? Hang out my shingle?

Dirty politics has been around since the first Neanderthals crawled down from their cold caves and formed the first village. Somebody had to be chief and it was usually the biggest, meanest son-of-a-bitch in the village, that is, until the smart little guy who invented the spear buried it between the shoulder blades of the big, mean son of a bitch. Lucy Sue with all her indignation and journalistic exposes wasn't going to change the nature of politics and greed. I sure as hell wasn't either, but then I wasn't going to try.

I liked being a chief administrative assistant in Washington and while Wiley's personal beliefs weren't mine, he was true to his. That was enough for me. I could deal with a foolish consistency, even if Mr. Emerson couldn't. If Aeriel was on the brink of a breakdown, then she needed to figure out how to live with her reality. Lucy could do her a favor and tell her not to give a shit about what people like Wiley think, but of course that wouldn't help much with the father. There wasn't anything to be done there. Intolerant bigoted assholes, like the poor, we will always have with us.

Still, reason and the reading of history are cold consolation to someone like Aeriel who is young and hasn't yet come to grips with her sexuality. I sure as hell couldn't help. Every time a situation like this raises its head, I think of something one of my clients in Warren said. "Life is just shit on rye, Billy, and everybody you meet is another bite."

A bit extreme yet a reasonable safety valve for me.

Occasionally, I saw him proven wrong, rare as that was, and that was good. But for the most part, every new person I met eventually unpacked his or her bag of trouble in front of me. Trouble was the natural state and Aeriel'd just have to learn to eat her sandwich or die starved.

"So, what are you gonna do?" I said.

"I'm gonna publish my article next week. It's gonna explain how Earl Anthony is using this show and these two artists to raise money for his machine. It's gonna say that Senator Wiley Hoots's campaign staff has concluded that the Xers' art show is a valuable tool for him to use in raising campaign money. And it's gonna tell my reader the human costs of these fundraising strategies."

"Lucy, you know that Earl and Wiley will both deny this. They'll say they're doing their duty to inform the public about the immoral use of taxpayers' money for an art show that mocks the moral underpinnings of this country. They'll say they don't care what deviants do within the confines of their own world just so long as the government doesn't help promote it. Why don't you just stick to the facts and not make this a crusade? Why don't you develop an article, not a speech?" Lucy got out of her chair. She walked to the edge of the porch, took a deep breath and slowly turned around.

"Why don't you develop a backbone? Why don't you stand for something other than going along to get along? I thought I was a cynic, but compared to you I'm Mother Teresa. Billy, I don't know your first wife and I don't really know your mom and dad, so I probably don't understand your foundations, but I thought I knew you. Now you're starting to scare me. I almost love you. 'Almost' because the more I think I know who William Walpole Bowater the Third is, the more I think I don't. Do you know who he is? Who he wants to be? If you do, then please tell me because I don't want to *almost* love you."

I knew we would get here. I knew that eventually we would be knocking at Billy's door, looking for answers. I didn't want to give an answer right now. The William Bowater I knew was smart, resourceful, witty, and cynical, but I wasn't sure he wanted to stand for something. I wasn't sure he was ready to put his arms around the holly tree.

"I will. I'll tell you when I know. We—me and William—are getting to know each other and when we're satisfied with who we are and where we're going, we'll tell you because we think we almost love you, too. I made a mistake my first time and maybe it was because that Billy didn't really understand or like that Billy. I don't know. Maybe I've seen too much. Maybe I'm a coward. Maybe, maybe, maybe . . . maybe we need to have a rum and go get some shrimp."

She smiled and nodded.

17.

"Goddammit, Billy, what the hell were you thinking of? Why didn't you stop him? And where the fuck were you, out getting coffee?" John Carter was shaking. Small rivulets of spit were appearing at the corners of his mouth. I was enjoying myself. It occurred to me that if I smiled, I might, just might, cause a minor thrombosis . . . so I smiled.

John's mouth opened without a sound. He was in utter disbelief. How could I smile at such a time? He regained his rage. "This is funny? You think that the destruction of the senator's campaign is funny? Maybe I should let Wiley in on the joke. 'Senator, good news, your AA thinks your episode last night was funny. What do you think?'"

He was right. It wasn't funny, and now John's hysteria wasn't funny either, just boring. I had come to his office at his insistence but was sorry I had indulged his obsession with Wiley's recent gaffe.

"The episode," I said, looking straight into John's eyes, "As you so spinningly put it, was not funny; however, your mindless hysteria does strike me as funny. So if you are now over your screaming and self-indulgent fulminations, perhaps we can discuss our situation more dispassionately." This seemed to have a calming influence.

145

The "episode" to which John was referring occurred the night before on a local TV program out of WRUL in Raleigh, "The State of Our State." The interview and call-in program gave the conservative host fifteen or twenty minutes to interview a public figure in North Carolina, then open the phone lines for questions. Wiley had been on the show dozens of times, his past affiliation with the station always being acknowledged.

Wiley and I went to the studio and I sat in a small adjoining office during the proceedings. Contrary to what John imagined, I was nowhere near any technical equipment or show engineers to manage any gaffe or insult of Wiley's. Everything had gone according to plan and just as in Wiley's previous appearances, the majority of the calls were kiss-ass declarations, not questions. Interspersed with these was the occasional liberal diatribe that Wiley dismissed with the usual admonishments—the caller being "un-American and anti-Christian." But near the end of the show, a man clearly of the redneck persuasion called in.

"Senator, I jus' wanna say that me and a lot of other God-fearing folks owe you a debt of gratitude. I know this ain't politically correct and all that, but I reckon you deserve one of them Nobel prizes for everything you done to he'p keep down the niggers. God bless you." Wiley, without any apparent hesitation replied, "Well, thank you!" and saluted the camera. The next second, the show's moderator said, "Oh, dear," and Wiley added, "My goodness, I mean, you know, that is not something that I think is appropriate to say, and I don't, uh, think I have ever been involved in something that detracts from a person's rights, uh, no matter what ethnic origin."

No one on the show had reacted fast enough to delete the caller's statement. It was a live broadcast and had already gone out, along with Wiley's response. John knew that there was nothing anyone could have done to stop it. He was simply pissed that it had happened and took it out on me.

The fact is, Wiley early in his career had been an unapologetic segregationist. He had publicly stated his opinions while employed at WRUL and had employed segregationist, scare tactics during numerous statewide and federal campaigns. Wiley used the term "nigger" often in his early non-political days; however, since running for office, he had cleaned up his act. Instead of his old epithets, he'd use code words like "Amos" in place of "nigger," "personal freedoms," "quotas," and "majority beliefs." These were the modern-day euphemistic equivalent of using the states-right argument to rally for the Civil War. The bigots didn't want to admit that pro-slavery attitudes had anything to do with the war, rather it had been a matter of "states' rights."

In any case, John Carter knew that Wiley's gaffe was huge. I didn't think it was that big a deal, but I did realize that it would have to be addressed. I wrote a response for the senator that said he was thinking about something else at the time and wasn't paying attention to the caller's offensive statement. At the end, he was simply thanking the man for calling in. He had, of course, never condoned that sort of language and certainly was never a proponent of any kind of racial bias or discrimination. His statement apologized by proxy for the caller's language and reiterated his unqualified rejection of the sentiments expressed. He in no way considered the caller's statement a compliment to him:

"Sentiments such as those expressed by the caller on last night's broadcast of 'The State of Our State' have no place in the civil discourse among citizens of this great state, and I am personally distressed at the affront this caused many of our fellow North Carolinians. I should have been paying closer attention to the caller rather than letting my mind wander." Blah, blah, blah. Wiley at least got some face time on most of the state's TV stations to refute the clip, which, of course, they also played.

But his escape was questionable. He got to express his indignation at the offensive language the caller employed, but still had his gratified face and his "Well, thank you!" response and salute broadcast over and over again.

The voters, at least those with an IQ above that of a house plant, knew that Wiley was a senior citizen, thus prone to having his mind wander on occasion. They, his loyal supporters, would give him the benefit of the doubt. That the Democrats might use this for some sort of attack ad was irrelevant—to me; however, not to John Carter. As usual, John figured he needed to make a new TV ad that would hit back at the other side when they employed—and he was sure they would—the "keeping-down-the-niggers" strategy. The fact that John made a huge amount of money for every ad the campaign shot was, of course, irrelevant.

The only part of his paranoia I agreed with was the possibility of Governor James' using the "senile" strategy—Wiley's TV gaff suggested that the senator was too old to represent North Carolinians because he was newly prone to having his mind wander. After all, Wiley was well over seventy years old and often came across on television as confused and a little scatterbrained.

As fate would have it, Governor James took the opposite approach. He created and aired an ad that referred to the "Well, thank you!" statement; however, what he implied was that contrary to Wiley's claims of having his mind wander, the Senator had heard exactly what the man said and answered quickly and candidly. Only after he realized the incendiary nature of what he had said, did he recant.

I tried in my own mind to come to the opposite conclusion; however, I could not. I have too often heard Wiley comment in ways that bordered on racism. I simply figured that this was one of the things I was hired to clean up after and spin. John Carter, on the other hand, was not only indignant about the governor's ad but prone to vindictive revenge against him. Even before the WRUL incident, John had looked for something personal to hang on Governor James, but he never could find any dirt or major public gaffe on a par with Wiley's.

The only thing he could come up with was to tie the governor to the Xers' show, depicting him as an endorser of government-sanctioned pornography and homosexuality. But Governor James's campaign deflected any responsibility and re-directed the onus to the NEA. The only thing John could accuse the governor of was that he didn't condemn the artists, the NEA, and Carolina, and that was feeble because it asked the public to take too many steps to reach a conclusion.

One ad said: "Even when shown the contents of this so-called 'art show' organized by the state of North Carolina at UNC, its leading institution of higher learning, along with the federal government through its notoriously indulgent agency, the National Endowment for the Arts, Governor James decided to side with those perverted, deviant artists and their enablers in academia. When is enough going to be enough? Do the citizens of this great state have to pay for even more pedophilia-inspired photographs and blasphemous, homoerotic paintings before they take action? Let's hope not." And so on and so on.

The first time I saw the new ad, Wiley, John Carter, Derrick Williams, John Carter's director of media, Hoover Leggett, and I were in a conference room just down the hall from our main office in Dirksen. John started the meeting with his rationale for a new ad, namely that we needed to strike at the personal belief system of Governor James just as he had done with his "Well, thank you!" ad against the senator. John's rationale was the same one he used every time . . . "This is war not peace," "Politics is a blood sport so expect to get bloody," "An eye for an eye," blah, blah, blah. After his preamble and rationale, he rushed to summary:

"So, gentlemen, I think we should modify the current lineup of ads and immediately insert the new ' values' ad into our schedule."

I looked around the room. Would there be no discussion of either the content or the timing of the ad?

"John, if I may. How do you know that the governor was shown the contents of this art show? I don't recall that he has ever said anything about the Ackland show except to say that the university in its educational mission had the complete trust of the citizens of North Carolina. That it wasn't the job of the governor to tell the university what it could teach, say, or inquire into."

"Exactly. He is giving up the bully pulpit so not to upset his money source among Chapel Hill grads. He's morally a coward."

"Yes, but that's not the same as siding with pedophiles, perverted deviants, and blasphemers. You're talking apples and oranges, John."

"Come on, Billy. You know as well as I that these wackos are just looking for publicity."

"As a matter of fact, I know that at least one of the wackos, Ms. Sopwith, who is an art instructor at East Carolina, was raised as a devout Baptist, and is a well-respected teacher and artist."

"And how do you know that? Your girl friend on the paper?"

I could feel the blood rising in my face. "Yes, the paper. You see, I actually read on occasion so that I can be informed rather than make shit up out of whole cloth in order to win at any cost. If you had read the extensive coverage of the Xers' show, you too could be informed about the facts. Unless, of course, the facts are of little interest to you, in which case we are hardly in a position to throw any moral stones at anyone else." Before I could continue, Senator Hoots interrupted.

"Gentlemen, this is getting us nowhere. Billy, you and I need to talk later this afternoon. Hoover, I appreciate your input and appreciate your coming to D.C. for the last few days to work on the campaign. I'll see you in Raleigh this weekend. John, I'll call you later and discuss what our schedule will be. Thanks, fellows." With that everyone stood up, gathered their papers and started down the hall to the elevator banks. I was the last to leave since I had to lock up. Wiley started out the door, then turned around.

"Since we're alone now, let's just have a little visit here." He came back in and sat at the head of the conference table. I took a chair two down from Wiley and waited.

"Son, I've told you before that I didn't care whether you agreed with me or not, but I don't think that's the whole truth. Your moral stand or lack thereof is starting to affect my trust in you. I realize I'm not your ordinary senator, but then I don't want to be. I believe that I was destined by God to be here and to be better than the rest of these political prostitutes.

"Being a man of faith has given me the ability to withstand the criticism of the go-alongs and the non-believers. And it is the lot of the true Christian to be attacked. We have been persecuted since the death of our Lord. I hate playing the mindless games of politics, and you know that, Billy. That's the main reason you're here, to do that for me. You also know that initially I brought you here as a favor to your daddy. It was only after you proved your administrative abilities and keen insights that I promoted you, but William, you are now starting to worry me.

"I don't understand how someone as smart as yourself can't understand the importance of this race and the danger of our situation. We both know the reality of politics—it isn't always pretty, but it is the reality that we have to live with. Linking Governor James with those two artists is good politics. If you don't want to call them deviates, don't, but that's what they are regardless of what you think.

"I call a spade a spade, and a perverted human being a perverted human being. It ain't normal, what they do. It ain't normal and it's destroying this country. Underlying everything I've done and everything I've said is this: We in this country are on a slippery slope in terms of morals and decency. And it's way past the time that we back up and say to ourselves, enough." He stopped. He squinted his eyes and stared at me, waiting. I kept my eyes on him, not wanting to give anything up. I thought, how hard do I get? Do I say what I think? I took a deep breath and exhaled.

"Senator, I appreciate the fact that you are a man of strong beliefs, and I take your word for the fact that your faith compels your actions; however, I am not a man of faith, at least a faith that you would claim. But this has never stopped me from working on your behalf since it is you who was elected, not me. I also understand the reality of politics. But senator, part of who you are is a morally conscious man, and for the life of me I can't understand how destroying another person's life—destroying Ms. Sopwith's and Mr. Pope's life—in order to win an election can be justified. Just because they are different from you and believe in different things than you doesn't mean they're against you." Wiley was by now on the edge of his seat. His mouth was taut and his eyes slits.

"I assume you're talking about those two deviates in that art show, so let's cut to the chase. I'm not the one destroying their life, they are. I'm not the one painting pictures of people urinating on other people or of Jesus kissing another man. I'm not the one portraying young naked girls hugging each other. You want forgiveness, ask God, not Wiley Hoots. Forgiveness is not mine to give. But I know that the Lord I love, the God I worship, has made it abundantly clear what he expects and what he demands of his children. If that Southwith woman asks Him to forgive her, and means it, He'll do it, because he is a loving God. But don't ask Wiley Hoots—he's just a man, a sinner who is trying to cope."

"Senator, I'm not asking for you to forgive these people. They don't seek your forgiveness. I'm asking that you not use them. I'm asking that they not be maligned for what they feel are legitimate artistic expressions. Why . . . ?" He raised his hand and cut me off.

"William, do I not have the same right of expression? Can I not say that I believe their 'artistic work' to be obscene and without social merit? I don't give a damn what they do in their life. I care that our government, that 'we the people' are not poisoned with our own money. You want to give them a show in a private gallery, go ahead. That's none of my business, but, by God, it is my business when they ask the people of this state and country to pay for their depravity!" He was trembling, and I needed to pull back some.

"Senator, I'm sorry. You make your point well, as always. Perhaps I'm trying too hard to see the good in people and not recognizing the bad. I believe these artists felt they were making a point. I believe that Ms. Sopwith is not a pedophile and that she is simply photographing what she believes are beautiful young girls. They are the nieces of a friend. And by the way, she didn't ask for the public's money, it was thrust upon her. All she did was submit her work to a jury of art experts.

"Blaming the NEA is a legitimate point of view since they were the initiators. In Ms. Sopwith's case, she just felt that the human body, which has been celebrated for hundreds if not thousands of years by artists of every sexual persuasion, was a legitimate artistic subject. I feel sorry for her. Her own father has turned against her because of what Earl and we have said. I don't . . ."

Wiley stood up. He took a deep breath and looked at me for a long moment.

"William, in spite of what you may think, I also try my best to see the good in people. But, son, there are boundaries that we may not cross. There are rules set down by God that are not optional or open for our approval. I'm sorry this young woman has strayed and if I could help I would, but I don't know what I can do. I believe that homosexuality is against God's will. This is not just a different lifestyle we're talking about here. This is sodomy. There are boundaries, William, and sometimes they have to be marked with a walking stick, not an ice-cream cone. Ms. Southworth can change, and she must if she is to receive His grace."

"Yes sir, I . . ." but before I could finish, Wiley turned and left. I could hear his footsteps clacking on the marble floor.

Leaning back in my chair, I closed my eyes. What the fuck was I doing here? How could I come so far yet feel so low? Ladies and gentlemen, may I introduce William Walpole Bowater the Third, scion of a great law practice, Morehead Scholar, lawyer, Administrative Assistant, drunk, and capitulating caffeine-addicted nicotine-sucking bureaucrat. Stand up, William, and take a bow. I stood up, took my pen and pad from the desk and walked back to my office among the crowd of other bureaucrats, wondering if any of them felt about themselves as I did about myself.

18.

It was 1:30 in the afternoon and I'd already been in the office for eight hours. Wiley was down in North Carolina shaking hands, eating barbeque and whipping up the troops. He needed to make sure that his voter base was prepared to turn out in force. To insure this, we were planning a major literature drop every Sunday from now until election-day. We had printed hundreds of thousands of sample ballots to be put on the windshields of cars in every parking lot of every church that would let us in. Suggested statements of support had been mailed to preachers in churches, large and small, all over the state.

The Christian Crusade had promised not only a series of mailings to both voters and donors, but also mailings of sample ballots to their members. As far as our own state campaign workers, we were at the hand-to-hand combat part of the war. Phone banks and knocking on doors was the gritty truth of it. While we were still running ads in every market, no new ads would be made—the message had to stand on its own.

Every poll, internal as well as external, had the race as a dead heat.

However, two national polls had Governor James ahead by five to six points. Naturally, Carter and Horton disagreed with these numbers, but Wiley was still worried. Regardless of the actual standings, the rhetoric had heated up.

To hear Wiley tell it the homosexuals were massing on our borders preparing to invade; the abortionists were planning new clinics to handle the crowds freed up by *Roe vs. Wade*; and soon every business would be audited by the federal government to make sure that they had the required number of minorities on their payroll.

Governor James's campaign was not much better. The only difference was in the language employed. The Democrats were more moderate in their choice of words, but more demeaning in their aspersions. The race pitted haughty arrogance against mean-spirited alley fighting.

It was hot outside. By noon the temperature had reached seventy-five degrees. Summer had hung around to claim the days, making fall a night visitor. I had lunch in the building cafeteria then took a short walk around the capitol grounds, so by 1:30, the day had caught up with me and I was feeling sleepy. I rested my feet on my windowsill and looked out at capitol square and the still-green trees that shaded its walkways.

I began to daydream about nothing in particular—law, love, and how the hell I got here. I thought about Sylvia and what fun we had had in Chapel Hill, what went wrong, and how I could have done things differently. I smiled thinking about Lucy Sue, how much fun she was, and how much she meant to me. I wondered what...

"Mr. Bowater, there's a call on line 1."

I shook my head to wake up, "Thank you, Ruth Lee."

"Hello."

"Billy, it's Felix Cooper. You got a minute?"

"Felix, for you I've got two minutes."

"Good. Listen, I'm in D.C. at the moment and wondered, I know it's kind of last minute, if you could have dinner tonight?"

"Well, Felix, unless you know something my doctor doesn't, I can have dinner every night." I loved to hear his spectacular laugh.

"Okay, would you like to have dinner with me? I have something I'd like to discuss with you."

"Of course. What time and where?"

"I'm staying at the Fairfax. What say we have dinner at the Jockey Club. It's on your way home and an elevator ride for me."

"I'll meet you at 7:30, okay?"

"Good. See you then."

My day was improving. I loved the Jockey Club. It was located in the Fairfax Hotel on Massachusetts Avenue in the consulate district. Every country in the world that wasn't at war with us had a gaudy mansion on the avenue housing either their ambassador or their consul. Within the district it was known as party central.

The Jockey Club wasn't on my list of places to stop for dinner since one dinner there cost as much five dinners at my usual haunts; however, when asked by a well-heeled lobbyist or faux lobbyist where I wanted to go—Jockey Club it was.

Felix was already seated at a discreet corner banquette when I got there. He was also half-way through what appeared to be a deep-dish dirty Martini.

"Yo, Mr. Cooper, I see that you began communion without me."

Felix held his usual long guffaw to a mild mini-burst.

"Only the blood. I was waiting to order the body until you finally showed." We shook hands and I turned to the waiter who was hovering nearby.

"How about a Macallan's on the rocks—fifteen year if you have it." Felix looked over the top of his glasses at me as I sat next to him in the banquette.

"Cute, but that's it. No paté or caviar for you tonight. Reverend Anthony is pretty strict about Washington expense accounts."

"Right, that's why you stay at the Fairfax and eat at the Jockey Club. Don't give me that shit, Felix. Earl flies around in a twenty-million-dollar jet and you're telling me he pisses about single malt scotch?"

"Okay, okay. But don't go crazy. He really does like to piss about little stuff sometimes. It makes him feel like he's back on the fried chicken circuit—like he's one of the people."

I smiled and held my tongue. Such hypocrisy made me want to gag.

"If it's not too much, Felix, I'd like to order the Steak Dianne. In fact, if you've never had it here, I highly recommend it." Felix smiled and said to the waiter, "Two."

We made small talk for ten or fifteen minutes. How's the campaign going? What did I think about the poll numbers? How was Wiley's health?

All of the bullshit said, it became clear that Felix was trying to get somewhere but couldn't find the right segue. To help out, I stopped talking, looked at him until he stopped, and then said, "Felix, clearly you have something on your mind other than Wiley's and my health. Rather than wasting time with niceties, why don't you just cut to the chase?"

He smiled, leaned back against the banquette and said, "Good idea. Okay, here it is. We're worried about this race. Ever since Wiley's meltdown on TV his numbers have been going south. When Earl heard a replay of that "keeping the niggers down" fiasco, he about blew a fuse. I mean, what the fuck was he thinking, Billy?"

I took a deep breath and stared hard at Felix. "Felix, it caught him by surprise. He wasn't expecting it. I mean, how could you? Some redneck comes out with something like that, nobody could expect that." Felix rolled his eyes.

"I understand, but 'thanks,' and a salute?"

"Look, Felix, it's done. Get over it."

"Yeah, well, easy for you to say. Earl doesn't quite see it that way. As you know, we're growing the Crusade by huge numbers and the 'niggers' as Wiley so cleverly I.D.'s them, are a big part of our growth plans."

"Wait a Goddamn minute! Wiley never said 'nigger'. He even apologized for the 'neck who did say it. Earl can't pin this on Wiley, he . . ."

"Stop, Billy. Stop right there. I believe there was a 'thanks' said in there. Maybe he didn't mean it, in fact, I'll give you that he didn't;

however, other folks don't see it that way. Our internal polls show that over sixty-five percent of those who saw the program or heard a replay, believe that Wiley said 'nigger.' "

"Anyway, one of the things I came to tell you is that we're modifying our mailings. We're still sending out the sample ballots, but we're not sending out crusade pamphlets endorsing Wiley per se. We're not saying anything negative, just not saying anything one way or the other. The sample ballots are national ones showing many candidates all over the country and Wiley's name is still checked on those."

I looked at him with what I hoped was a disgusted but un-emotional expression. "Okay, I guess I know where we stand with the Christian Crusade."

Felix shook his head. "Come on, Billy. You know damn well this kind of thing can kill us. We're still friends of Wiley's, but for now we need to let this go away. I mean what would you do if you were in our place. Endorse his salute?"

"Of course not. I would say that after talking to the senator, you, meaning Earl, believe that he was shocked and taken by surprise. You can distance yourself from the sentiment without abandoning Wiley."

"Yes, we could, but right now it's just too fresh. Still, I'll talk to Earl about a statement like the one you just mentioned. Given a little distance, he might buy that. You know how much he thinks of Wiley."

"Yeah, I do now."

Felix gave me his best oh-come-on-pal look, then took another drink. "Okay, off the campaign and on to the next subject, and the most important."

I held up my hand. "Wait a minute. I've got something that I want to say before we leave the campaign." Felix looked annoyed but not surprised.

"As a favor to me, stop the bullshit attacks on those two poor artists in the Ackland show."

Now Felix looked surprised. "What the hell for?"

"Because they haven't done anything to deserve it. All they did was submit their art to a jury of academics to see if they could win a little money and be included in an exhibit at the university museum. All this deviate and pervert language is starting to hurt them and possibly endanger them."

"Jesus, Billy. Tell 'em it's just politics. It'll be over in month or so. I mean. . . ."

"Hey, back up! You're fucking us on the mailings—you owe me."

He smiled and nodded. "Fine. We've about milked that show for all it's worth, anyway."

~

Felix drained the last of his martini, then looked around the room to see if anyone was near enough to listen or looked like they might want to.

"Let's play what if, okay?"

I picked up my second Macallan's, followed his look around the restaurant, then said,

"Okay, let's."

He settled back in the leather of the banquette and looked at me as if he was deciding whether to reveal a secret. "Billy, I'm gonna tell you some things and I want your word that nothing I say will go further than this booth. I won't put you on the spot. I won't ask you to betray any trust with Wiley or anyone on his campaign. But I want to talk to you about you and your future.

"If you feel at any time that I'm treading on something you're uncomfortable with, let me know, okay?"

I nodded and added, "Okay, but let's agree that *everything* said here tonight is just between us." Felix smiled and nodded his agreement.

"Let's say," Felix said, "the senator loses his race. Not that he will, but let's just say that he does, for argument's sake. What's next for William Walpole Bowater the Third?" I started to say something but he held up his hand. "If you don't mind, let me finish my whole story before you say anything, okay?" I agreed.

"Well, there are other senators to work for. You have a lot of experience; you're smart; you're alert, have contacts, know how to play the game on the hill. But what else is out there? You can be a bag man on K Street. Take congress people out to eat at The Jockey Club and the

Congressional Golf Club. You can practice law in North Carolina at Bowater & Bass LLC., a prestigious law firm. Or, you could be the executive director of The Center for Cultural Traditions or CCT.

"If you're racking your brain to recall what it does or where you've heard the name, don't. It doesn't exist, yet. That's why I'm here. Earl and I, mainly I, along with some very, and I do mean very, wealthy backers, are looking to start a new research institute in Washington. Not that Washington needs a new think tank, but CCT, if we get it right, won't be like the others.

"We plan on having a think tank more along the lines of the Abrams M1 tank as opposed to the weak-ass academic groups that currently populate the field. In a nutshell, CCT will take its place on the international stage along with organizations like The American Enterprise Institute, The Cato Institute, The Heritage Foundation, and other similar right-wing research organizations.

"While we haven't fully defined the mission statement and organization chart, what we want to do is buy a seat at the conservative table in Washington without sticking 'evangelical' in everybody's face. The truth is that most of these research organizations are just fronts for a particular political bias. They decide on the results they want, then finance studies to get those results. It's sort of a ready-fire-aim approach to research. Both parties get the majority of their position statements from the think tanks that are on their side.

"As I said, CCT won't have anything in its mission statement about being evangelical, but will accumulate data and names that will be very helpful to evangelical organizations such as the Christian Crusade. Money buys information and information is power. You think that could pass for our mission statement, Billy?"

I didn't say anything. My eyes and expression spoke for me.

"I don't think so, either. Anyway, you get the picture. So, what do you think? Oh, before you answer, one more thing. The average salary of a CEO of one of the big think tanks is somewhere between five hundred thousand and a million dollars a year, plus car and benefits."

What did I think? Shit, I couldn't make that much money at home without a gun. Who could think? I needed to be cool. I needed to look like I was interested but not overly impressed.

"Well, as you can imagine, I have lots of thoughts. I understand where you are, so I won't ask questions you can't reasonably have answers for. One question that you can answer is—why that name?"

"Good first question. Billy, the crusade has interests in many places. Our international broadcasting division is incorporated in Panama, but with offices in Washington and Atlanta. Our travel and software companies are incorporated in Bermuda with offices in Liechtenstein, New York, and Atlanta. The world has gotten smaller, and we need to be alert to the cultural differences of our members and potential members all over the world. Our proposed name is innocuous, it's classy sounding, it's academic, and it's non-partisan.

"As I've said, we don't need another evangelical lobby on the hill. We need the assistance of moderate legislators which we won't get unless we're viewed as a non-partisan institute. The truth is, of course, more malleable. You won't be involved in the international investments and interests of the crusade because there will be no formal ties between CCT and the crusade, but wearing other hats you may become an 'advisor' to Earl and me."

"Okay. Why me?"

Felix smiled as he motioned to the waiter.

"Another good question, but first, a brandy. Two Courvoisier Napoleons, please, waiter."

The brandies arrived and Felix, in a fit of pseudo-sophistication, swirled and sniffed the rarefied liquid as if he actually knew what the hell he was doing.

"Since there is still much to be done, Earl and I decided that what we needed as a founding CEO was a brilliant lawyer with a strong academic background, a man with a great deal of experience in the Washington stone crusher, and a person with a flexible moral compass."

My eyes narrowed at that. "Well, thank you for the brilliant lawyer part, but I'm afraid I must disagree with the flexible moral compass part."

Felix swirled his brandy and looked inside the snifter.

"I don't mean dishonest, Billy. In fact, I know that you would never do anything to break the law; however, like me, your job is sometimes to bend it until you hear cracking—bend, don't break. We both work for men who fancy themselves messengers of God and whether they are or not is not our concern. Our job is to help them maintain their illusions, thus their power.

"As you pointed out to me in New Orleans, your and my stays there are not necessarily pious excursions, our evenings dedicated to salvation. You run Senator Hoots' professional life to keep him, and thus yourself, in power, just as I do for Reverend Anthony. We don't need to agree with them to work for them. I want a seat at the power table in Washington, too, and I want you to help me design our chair."

I sniffed the subtle bouquet of my cognac, and realized that it was the only subtle thing at the table. Felix had nailed me pretty well, and I could see he was enjoying the moment, but I didn't feel complimented or collegial. We weren't in this together. I was being compromised and needed to buy some space.

"Doesn't sound very grand when you put it that way, Felix. Sounds like we're picking up our money from the top of the dresser as we leave the room."

Felix laughed. "You could put it that way, but the truth is, and you know this as well as I, everybody in Washington is paid that way. How much campaign money have you given to legislators based on a wink and a nod? How much money has the senator taken from sources where he knows full well what they expect for their donation? Like your buddy Robert Fitzpatrick said, 'Billy doesn't mind swimming in a pool of shit as long as he can get out now and then.'"

I did a double take. "When the hell did you talk to Robert, and what for?"

"I didn't, but one of our major donors is a client of Jinthum & Fandors. He was talking to Mr. Fitzpatrick and some of his associates about a problem he had in Washington and your name came up. Our donor simply inquired about one William Walpole Bowater, and your friend, and he is your friend, gave you glowing kudos. He said that you were cut out for Washington; that you knew how to play the game; that you were the smartest legal mind he knew and hungry to prove yourself away from North Carolina."

Too bad I used the "swimming in pools of shit" analogy with Robert, but it could have been worse. It was time to keep my mouth shut and think. I needed to get out of here. We finished our brandy, made some more small talk, but the business part of our dinner was over. I looked at my watch and slowly stood up. We shook hands. More hypocrisy. "Felix, thank you. I'll obviously need to give this a lot of thought. I'll have questions, and . . ."

"No rush, Billy. As I said, we're just formulating our plans, and we know you're in the middle of a tough campaign. Keep us in mind. If this opportunity is of interest, then it doesn't really matter whether Wiley wins or not. The job could still be yours."

I smiled. "Thanks. Thank you for thinking of me. I'll give this serious thought and be back in touch, but not in the next couple of weeks—you understand. And, by the way, I'll tell the senator how you and Earl feel about the mailings. My guess is that he'll want to talk to Earl about that pretty soon."

Felix nodded and smiled. "I'm sure."

I walked out of the hotel and into the cool night air. The traffic on Massachusetts Avenue was light so my trip home would be short. I turned and started walking to my car a block away.

A law bender? A shit-pool swimmer? Goddammit, a law bender? How many Bowaters have been law benders? Fuck.

19.

November was upon us. I had spent the last two weeks shuttling between Raleigh and the other cities in the state looking for every last campaign dollar. Both sides had by now thrown every dirty punch, every jagged-edged brick they had money to buy. The polls hadn't changed much. The senator was still even with the governor, but John Carter and his bevy of number crunchers believed, or wanted to believe, that among likely voters Wiley was ahead. Our campaign spending was estimated to be near or just above twenty million dollars.

I had seen Lucy only a few times over the past month. Hardly surprising since she was busy covering the election for the *N&O*, and I was traveling all over the state looking for money and endorsements. It was now twelve days before the election and Wiley had decided to take the weekend off to rest before the final push. He and Earl had reached a compromise on the crusade's participation, so all that was left to do was a last-minute tour of the state. But that would be next week, not this weekend. This meant that I too could take a little personal time, so I called Lucy from our Durham campaign office.

"Luce, I'm in Durham and was hoping that we could have dinner tonight."

"Who is this?"

"Very funny. You know I've been out of town for the past few weeks. Don't bust my chops, Lucy. I really want to see you." I could hear her smile, or at least I told myself so.

"Okay, where do you want to go?"

"I don't care. You choose. I'll even pick you up at your place. How's that for service?"

"Be still, my heart. I have to finish some work here, so how about eight o'clock? You're the inviter so you pick."

"Eight it is."

I was speechless. I knocked, the door opened and there stood Lucy Sue Tribble in a dress. Not only a dress but a really pretty dress and makeup and high heels and jewelry.

"Oh, uhm, excuse me, Mrs. Tribble, but is Lucy here? We have a date tonight and I told her I would pick her up at eight."

"Screw you! I dress up, put on a little perfume, my entire jewelry box, and all you can do is give me shit?"

I laughed out loud. "Forgive me, Ms. Tribble. I'm surprised and a bit overwhelmed, but let me say that you look and smell beautiful. You are what dreams are made of."

Lucy smiled, patted me on the cheek and said, "Good recovery. Tonight may be your night."

I had made reservations at one of the newest and best-reviewed restaurants in the Triangle. It was in an old textile factory converted into an upscale shopping mall and office complex. While Lucy protested that this was far too extravagant, she was nonetheless pleased that I had thought of it. To set the proper tone, I ordered a bottle of old, very fine Bordeaux; this to accompany a generous serving of paté-de-foie gras for two, followed by equally delectable entrées. Fact is, we both needed something special tonight, something different from our usual workday fare of steaks and fries.

The conversation was as smooth as the wine. We traded campaign stories, candidate gossip, and generally talked trash without incident. I made sure not to mention anything about the Xers' exhibit or its aftermath. If that was to become a subject, then Lucy would have to raise it. About halfway through our main course, veal Oscar, Lucy looked up and smiled.

"I brought something that I thought might amuse you. You remember that I told you about my call with Christian Pope's gallery and that Donnovan fellow?"

"Yeah. I recall that it wasn't very productive."

"Well, about two weeks ago I got a letter from Mr. Pope. Too late for my article but interesting nonetheless." She handed me a single sheet of folded stationary.

Donnovon Gallery
124 15th St., N.W.
Washington, DC

Dear Ms. Tribble:

Robert told me you called a few weeks back. I believe he told you that I have no intention of engaging either Senator Hoots or the good Reverend Anthony in a debate about my work, the quality of the Ackland show, or the value of the National Endowment for the Arts. While I believe this might prove to be an interesting experience and a debate I would win hands down, nonetheless, I must refuse. The truth is that neither of the two aforementioned gentlemen wants a debate, they simply want to use images of my work to shake money out of their Nazi brothers.

As far as facts about myself, here are a few.

1. I am black, but not one of the niggers that the senator heped keep down.
2. I am male.
3. I am a artist, a damn good one.
4. I live in Washington, D.C.
5. I was born here and went to parochial schools for my early education.
6. I was not raped by a priest, but know some who were.

7. I did not know my parents since they died when I was very young.
8. The foster home in which I spent much of my youth could serve as a textbook example of a dysfunctional environment.
9. My sexuality is none of your fucking business.

I was nominated for the Ackland show by the faculty of American University and chosen by a prominent jury. I have tried drugs, smoked cigarettes, drunk copious quantities of alcohol, and masturbated. I am clearly not blind and do not have hairy palms.

My life story is totally irrelevant to whether I am a good painter. In fact, I believe I am an outstanding painter who may someday be a great painter. History, Ms. Tribble, not Wiley Hoots or Earl Anthony, will be my judge.

Regards,

Christian Pope

When I finished reading, I refolded the letter and handed it back to Lucy. "That's gotta be the best letter ever. You talk to the guy yet?"

Lucy shook her head. "Unfortunately, no. This letter is the only thing I've ever gotten from him. A month ago, when I met with Ginna Humphreys, she would say only so much about the artists' personal lives, and in the case of Christian she confessed that she didn't really know that much." Lucy looked around the restaurant to see if anybody was showing any interest in our conversation, quiet as it was.

"Ginna guessed that he was probably on the upper end if not beyond the X generation qualification dates. In any case, she said the faculty at American and Mr. Donnovon were so enthusiastic about Christian that he was included anyway in the pool of entrants. She said that the jury was really taken with his work and that if there had been an overall winner, he would have been a shoe-in.

"Aeriel was another matter. Ginna said that photographers always had a harder row to hoe since most jurors are biased toward the traditional arts of painting, sculpture, and print-making. She is also very fragile. Ginna said that prior to the show's opening, she spoke to Aeriel more often than to any other artist in the show. She has also spoken to her almost every week since the show closed. She agrees with me that

Aeriel is on the verge of a breakdown."

"Listen, Lucy. This whole damn election is gonna be over in less than two weeks. Only twelve days and then all these folks can get back to their lives . . . including me."

"And what is it you are gonna be getting back to, Billy?"

I smiled my "I-don't-want-to-get-into-this-right-now" smile. That's the one where I go rigid, my eyes look through you, and my mouth makes not the slightest attempt to speak.

Lucy waited then said, "Am I correct in assuming that you have just given me your 'shut-the-hell-up-about-this' look?"

"Yes."

"And do you think for a minute that I will accept that look?"

"Yes."

Lucy smiled and pushed her chair back from the table far enough so that she could cross her legs. "Fair enough. Can you read my body language?"

She had me there. "Lucy, come on. I've been busting my chops for the past six months on this campaign. I haven't liked a lot of it but it's my job. We haven't done anything illegal. We haven't broken any laws. We haven't done anything that everyone else hasn't done. What do you want from me?"

"I want from you what I know is there. I want you to believe in what you do. I want you to not be proud of simply not breaking the law." I wondered how she might feel about bending, but decided not to chance it.

"Lucy, for the most part, I believe in what I do, but am starting to lose faith in who I do it for. I'm thinking that Wiley's consistency is not just foolish, but mean. You want to know what I'm gonna do after election night? Okay... I don't know, but I've been looking at some interesting options."

"Like what?"

"I can't say, but take it from me that they're very interesting."

She got a disgusted look on her face. "And you can't tell me?"

"I can, but I may not. I had to promise that I wouldn't discuss it with anyone, so I haven't told anybody, but when I do, you will be the first. I'm not trying to be cute. The job is serious but I'm not sure it's me."

"Meaning you don't like the people or you don't like the job?"

"Maybe neither or maybe both."

She rolled her eyes, then tried a new line of inquiry. "You and Wiley have problems?"

"Let's just say that the senator and I have recently had a number of . . . of lively discussions concerning the whole morals, faith, integrity thing. He feels I have none of the above and I feel that those he has are fucked. Clear enough?"

Lucy smiled and nodded. "Well, maybe after this is over, you can try something else. Maybe you can find something that you love more than the D.C. power trip. Maybe your mystery 'opportunity' will be the ticket."

"Maybe."

"You going back to D.C. before election night?"

"Yeah, probably for a few days, then back here for the final week. You coming to the hotel on election night?"

Lucy took a bit of veal and smiled. "Doubt it. Unless we have been assigned to a specific candidate, we usually stay in the newsroom. The whole staff, including Mr. Frank, watches the results on different TV sets. The newsroom looks like a sports bar with six or seven TVs spread around. We yell at the sets, insult the candidates and commentators, throw spit balls at the screens, and generally act like left-wing crazies. You'd hate it."

"Quite the contrary. I love yelling at TVs, insulting candidates, throwing spit balls and acting crazy. Just so long as you and your left-wing crazies truly believe in free speech and the right of disagreement."

Lucy rubbed her chin. "I'm not sure that open-mindedness is tolerated by the press. We're a pretty closed-minded bunch."

I poured the last of the wine and leaned back. "Lucy, I will promise you one thing. After the election we'll spend some time together, and if you want to preach to me I'll listen."

She chuckled. "I ain't the preaching kind, William. All you gotta do is listen to yourself. That's where the answers are."

20.

What was that? I didn't know that sound. My head was throbbing, my mouth and throat dry. What time was it? Shit, what day? It stopped. Thank you, Jesus.

It started again. I turned over, pulling the pillow over my head, and yelled, "No one's here. Call back later," but it kept on ringing. Phone, my phone. Goddammit, who is calling at . . . early, anything before one P.M. Wiley's celebration party had lasted until daylight, which meant I hadn't gotten to my room until around eight.

As usual, Wiley wasn't assured of victory until after midnight. It always took a long time for the returns from the rural counties, those that still count ballots by hand, to come in. But these being the most conservative voters, their results were the most important and always provided his margin of victory. True to form, his winning margin was perhaps two percent, about what the polls predicted. Wiley's acceptance speech was his standard fare.

"The citizens of North Carolina have spoken, and again they have resoundingly opted for a government that will deliver what they want and need for themselves and their families. A government that respects the family values of a Christian society, a society that shuns the secular acceptance of depravity and moral decay. Let me again pledge to you, the citizens of this great state, that I, Wiley Grace Hoots, will never back down. I will continue to fight against the agents of moral decay, government waste, and social reconstruction."

It went on for about twenty minutes. I counted the number of people present at the end—couldn't have been more than a hundred. Down substantially from the five hundred or so that were in the hotel at the start of the evening. Aside from the media types who were covering the event, the crowd had been comprised of contributors who were either curious about an election night party or eager for Wiley and the rest of us on the staff to notice that they were there. I probably had fifty drunken sycophants come up to me at different times and say something like, "I knew our boy could do it, Billy. I was there all along and have been for every election. If I don't get to see him tonight, you tell Wiley that ole Jim Bob Wooten was here to push him over the finish line." It was pitiful. Jim Bob probably volunteered at one of the Hoots offices and or gave a couple hundred dollars and expected to get a personal letter from the Senator. I was tempted to say to some of these bozos, "Pal, unless your check was over ten grand, go to the back of the bus."

The Washington staff had a brief meeting with Wiley after his acceptance speech and just before he left at one A.M. for home. It was pointless since most of the staff was drunk and Wiley was so tired he didn't make a whole lot of sense anyway. He congratulated himself and all the little people who helped carry his water. Those weren't exactly his words but between the lines that was the message. His parting comments to me were a bit more coherent.

"William, I know that we haven't always seen eye to eye on some of our strategies during the campaign. The experience of working on a national campaign with professionals like John Carter and Willis Horton has been good for you though, given you understanding of how campaigning works in this country. I appreciate your long hours and hard work. I'm gonna take a few weeks off to be with Evvie and the grandkids, so you handle the Washington office." I thanked him and then asked when he wanted to start business on a regular basis.

"We need to function fully within two weeks. Of course, we have Thanksgiving and Christmas coming up so we'll have the regular holiday schedules. We should have most people in the office by Monday to answer calls from constituents. You don't have to be there until then. Take the rest of the week off but make sure that Larry has enough people in the office tomorrow to cover the bases. You keep in touch with him and call me only if something is really urgent." I smiled and again congratulated him on his victory, a goodnight kiss on the cheek always being appropriate. It's just that the cheek in question was far south of the one kissed by Evvie and the grand kids.

⁓

The ringing had stopped, but before I could get back to sleep I heard banging on my door. Now I was really getting pissed. I rolled out of bed, put on a T shirt, and went to the door.

"Who the fuck is it?"

"Billy, it's Lucy."

"Hold on." I slid the security chain out and unlocked the door, standing behind it as it opened.

"What the hell is going on, Lucy? What time is it, anyway? My head is killing me."

"One o'clock."

"Jesus! I didn't . . . One, really? I, uh, it's later than I thought. I knew it was light . . . What's all the fuss about." I went into the bathroom, splashed some water on my face, and looked around for my pack of Camels.

"Lucy, you got a cigarette?"

"It's a no-smoking room, Billy."

"So? Don't smoke. I'll do it for both of us." My head really hurt. I lit the cigarette, sat down on the bed and picked up the phone.

"Room service? Could you send a pot of coffee, some . . . you want anything?" She shook her head. "Some rolls and a large orange juice to Room 405. Thank you."

Lucy sat down on the bed while I looked for my pants. I put them on and turned around to face her. Something was wrong. Her face was ashen with splotches of red under her eyes from crying. I walked over, sat down beside her, and put my hand on her shoulder. This was no time for cute one-liners.

"What's wrong?"

She stared at me unfocused, like she was in shock. "She's dead, Billy. Aeriel is dead."

My face flushed and the heat rose and spread out. "When? How?"

"Sometime early this morning. And how? She hanged herself. About an hour ago I got a call from her partner, Fiona Welch, who said she'd gone by the house early this morning to fix breakfast and see how Aeriel was and . . . " She stopped and tried to catch her breath, tearing up. I'd never seen Lucy so upset, not even with me.

"Luce, you couldn't know. There was nothing . . ."

"No, Billy! Don't try to soothe over this as if she was an inanimate object that fell and broke—collateral damage in a fake, trumped-up war of words. Aeriel was a vulnerable human being who called me and confided in me and begged me for help. I should have done something, gone to see her, sat with her, something. I was AWOL."

"Lucy, you're a reporter. You aren't a player in her life; nor are you a shrink. You aren't any more responsible for what she does than you are for what the, the head of the DMV does. You observe and report, that's all." I stood and walked across the room, then turned and faced her. She watched me and for the first time since I had known her, I saw something unpredictable and angry in her eyes.

"I guess he's wrong," she said.

I sat back down. "Who's wrong?"

"John Donne. He's wrong. There is 'a man who is an island entire of itself.' His name is William Bowater and apparently for him the bell never tolls. You think, Billy, that my calling her and writing an article about her, including her family's reactions, didn't contribute to her shame and humiliation? You think I'm not guilty of the crimes of omission and commission? I told you she was on the edge. She confided in me because she believed that I was with her, that I was involved in mankind. I let her down. *I* did."

"Lucy, you thought she was heading for some kind of breakdown, not suicide. You didn't know her, not really. Yes, you told me that the campaign, that I, should try and stop the constant derogation of her character, her lifestyle—I tried. But until a few weeks ago I got nowhere, and apparently then it was too late—the campaign had Aeriel and Christian on its fast track to election-day. I wasn't part of the end game. I couldn't protect her any more than I could protect Christian Pope—and he got treated worse.

"Lucy, she was fragile and delicate, and delicate people don't have much chance in this world, that's just reality. I'm sorry. I'm truly sorry, but—" Lucy got up and wiped her face. She went into the bathroom and shut the door. I heard the water from the faucet and waited. The door opened and Lucy came into the room. She waited for a moment then said, "I'm going to the funeral. I'm told it might be Monday, but that isn't confirmed. It doesn't matter; I'm going and I'm gonna apologize to Aeriel and Fiona. Perhaps I can write something this time that honors her. Fiona blames herself. She spent last night at her sister's. She said that Aeriel called her after Wiley's victory speech and said something like 'Now that he has won, it will never stop. They've dragged me into history and can flip to my page anytime they want. "Who was that dyke in the '90 election?" And there I'll be, over and over.'"

Lucy walked over to the window, looked out, then turned and looked at me, but without the anger that had been in her eyes just minutes before.

"Fiona said she told Aeriel to get some rest and that she'd be home in the morning. She got there around six-thirty and went straight to the kitchen to fix breakfast. Even though she was usually up by then, Aeriel was nowhere to be seen. Fiona figured she was still sleeping, so she made herself coffee and read the paper. After about forty-five minutes when Aeriel hadn't come out, Fiona went to wake her. She said that, 'I needed to talk with her for my own sake.' She looked in the bedroom but Aeriel wasn't there; so, she went out back, to Aeriel's studio.

"When she opened the door, she saw her. She had hanged herself from the ceiling—from the pipes. Totally naked. She . . ." Lucy was sobbing.

I got up and put my arms around her, holding her fast against my chest. I patted her head and whispered into her hair. "It's okay. Don't cry. It'll be all right," knowing that it wasn't okay, that she couldn't stop crying, and that it wouldn't be all right. After a few minutes, Lucy cleared her throat, anger—probably for both of us—now in her eyes.

"As a final act of humiliation, Aeriel wrote across her chest in large red letters, letters, according to Fiona, made with her own blood, 'Pervert.' Can you imagine, Billy? Can you imagine cutting your fingers so deep they become fountain pens of blood? An interesting way to refer to oneself, don't you think? I wonder why she chose 'pervert'? That wouldn't be my choice. It's kind of old fashioned, huh? Why did she choose it to refer to herself?

"Ah yes. She must have read the newspapers recently and decided to use the same word used by those fine Christian gentlemen, Anthony and Hoots, the boys with a remedy, who have been flogging her of late. The word so profitably reported by the media, the enablers of those gentlemen!

"So I'm sure the good Reverend Anthony will be proud he has driven another sinner from our midst permanently. Each one sent to the nether regions makes us stronger, more clean and pure. The remedy for America's ills, Billy!

"And your boss, the saintly Senator Hoots, Defender of the Faith, I bet he's gonna be pleased. Get this, Billy. Fiona found a camera on a tripod on the other side of the studio. It seems that Aeriel set it up to photograph her death automatically. Perhaps Earl can buy the time-stamped series of photos to send in a newsletter to his major donors. They should be pleased their contributions have yielded such effective results. I bet the witch-dunkers-and-burners in Salem weren't any prouder."

"Lucy, no one is gonna get any pleasure out of . . ."

"Shut the fuck up! Don't say anything. Let me finish." She took a breath while I sat helplessly on the bed, knowing I didn't own the words to comfort her.

"Fiona asked me what she should do with the camera and while

I wanted to say that she should destroy it, I told her that it might be important to the authorities. She also found a letter addressed to her, so I told her not to read it to me or to show it to Aeriel's parents. If the police inquired about a suicide note, then she would have to decide what to do with it.

"But whatever she decides, I know nothing about any letter. If there is something in it that needs to be told to family or friends, then it's up to Fiona. That's probably not the advice I should give as a reporter, but I don't give a shit." She cleared her throat, ran her fingers through her hair, then stepped back and looked into my eyes.

"I suppose I'm not surprised you feel no responsibility for any of this. You've made no secret of the fact that you see yourself as a by-stander to life's parade. That is so refreshing, so lucky. I should envy your detachment, Billy, but I don't. Today is a horror because of Aeriel's loss, and I feel shitty for her and for my failure to help.

"I'm broken-hearted and a mess right now, but the joys and pains of being human, of making mistakes and being truly sorry for them, of having triumphs, then celebrating are natural and good.

"In the Bowater world you don't need to apologize or celebrate because the mistakes and triumphs are someone else's. How does it go? 'He's the one the people elected, not me. I'm the assistant, I assist.' I can see it now, Billy, etched there on your headstone: Here lies William W. Bowater the Third. He assisted." She smiled her don't-call-me-I'll-call-you smile, snorted in my direction, and left.

I stood there in the middle of my Hilton non-smoking double room, wearing a pair of smelly scotch-splashed pants and a sweaty T-shirt, holding a burned out Camel and knew Lucy was right. Everything she had thrown had stuck.

21.

By two-thirty I was clean—showered, changed into a clean suit, and gotten hold of Wiley at his home. He was none too pleased to have his afternoon interrupted. Had I not been so insistent, I don't think he would have seen me. But I was and so he would.

Evvie opened the door and invited me in. "Hello, William. I'm sorry if you have had a distressful day, but it will get better. Would you like something to drink? A coke, maybe, or tea?"

"No thank you, Mrs. Hoots. I'm fine."

"All right, but if you get thirsty just let me know. The senator is in his study. You know the way."

I walked down the hall and stood outside the study door to gather myself, then knocked.

"Come in, William." Wiley was sitting behind his desk with his hands crossed over his stomach. He gave the effect of a sleeping bear I'd just awakened. I sat down in the chair across the desk from him and waited. Wiley didn't move a muscle. He didn't smile, didn't frown, didn't do anything. I felt like a little mouse hunkered down in front of a coiled snake. Finally the mouse broke the silence.

"Senator, I think we have to say something about this, uhm, this event. It's not just that Ms. Sopwith killed herself, though this is a great tragedy, but how she killed herself. She chose a rather gruesome manner, hanging herself, naked, after painting the word 'Pervert' across her chest. In her own blood, sir. There is no doubt that the press will tie this event to our campaign as well as to the attacks by the Christian Crusade. While . . ." Wiley uncrossed his hands and held them forward and apart, palms up.

"What does this possibly have to do with us? We, the Reverend Anthony and our campaign, simply deplored the denigration of our Christian culture by artists supported by the university and the National Endowment. Anyone in this country is allowed to express their opinion, even U.S. senators and preachers. I am sorry that this poor, misguided child chose to end her life in such a horrible way, but that is the result of a life gone astray, not the result of anything said by me or by Reverend Anthony. We . . ." I could not restrain myself.

"Senator, you know that's not true. That woman never in her life, not once before she was chosen by the jury for the Xers' show, displayed any sign of depression. She never attempted suicide. She was by all accounts a pleasant, productive member of society. She was a respected teacher and photographer. She held a responsible position at East Carolina, in fact, one of our state's major institutions of higher learning. Perhaps she took all the criticism of her work too hard. Perhaps she was sensitive and too fragile to withstand the publicity, but she was not misguided—or evil."

Wiley had narrowed his eyes and his mouth was set hard and tight. He had re-crossed his arms, waiting for me to finish. I realized I was breathing more rapidly than usual and that my face was flushed and my mouth dry. I sat back, never taking my eyes off of his face and waited, I can't say how long.

He took a deep breath, then spoke. "William, perhaps we have finally reached an impasse. First, don't ever tell me what I know and what I don't know. What I know to be true and what I don't. I am older than your father and have been in this world forty years longer than you, so I can understand the passions of a young man as well as his frustrations, but I will not be lectured to. I will not be told 'You know that's not true.'

"What you don't know, because you have not yet been held accountable, is that we, we sinful human beings, are in fact held accountable. Held accountable by the power that created us, by our God, and whether you agree with that or not, that is the truth. And if you don't agree, then you're living in a dream.

"I am charged by God, as are the Reverend Anthony and many other devout Christians, to explain this truth: that human beings have a course and direction in life, a list of responsibilities and obligations, and that these have been revealed to us in his word . . . the Holy Bible. It is not now fashionable in many quarters to recognize and live by this code, but it never has been.

"Devout Christianity is a way of life for the strong, not the weak. God has given us everything we need to find him, his holy word and boundaries to mark our way. His boundaries are true and firm, laid out in the Bible as clearly as if by a holly tree planted on a property line. Compromise is the devil's way out.

"I'm too tired to try and explain this further. You are right that the press in their unceasing effort to sensationalize everything to sell newspapers and keep their jobs will take this tragic event and try to blame it on me and the crusade. But they will not succeed.

"They will rouse the passions of many against us, but they try to do that anyway. They will also catch the attention of our supporters. Everything I say is ridiculed by the left-leaning press, and this event will be no different. The thing is that the people who elected me, for now the fourth time, don't care what they say. They didn't vote for me to back away from my beliefs. On the contrary, they voted for me because of my beliefs.

"What you need to do is decide what you believe, William. Whether you can be a part of our team—or not." He stood up and moved around the desk until he was standing beside the chair I had now abandoned. We stood facing each other.

He held out his hand, "And you need to decide before Monday where you shall lie down and with whom." I took his hand and looked at him.

"I will, sir, but if I may, I'd like to come to Washington on Wednesday, not Monday."

"Why?"

"Because I'd like to attend the funeral of Ms. Sopwith which I believe is on Monday."

"That's a very bad idea, William. You will certainly be forced to say something to the press on my behalf and I won't permit that."

"Sir, I don't intend to be visible at the event nor will I speak to anyone from the press."

"Don't be foolish, Billy. Your friend Ms. Tribble is bound to be there and she will clearly demand some statement, and if you don't give her one, she will say that we are unresponsive."

"No, sir. I have already spoken to her and said that I cannot and will not make any statement of any kind. She has agreed. In fact, I haven't told her that I'm thinking of going to the funeral. I would guess, however, that she will try and contact you."

"I'm sure she will. I'll have Larry make a statement for the campaign. But back to this funeral idea. Why do you feel so compelled to go?"

"So that I can decide . . . where I must lie down and with whom."

For the first time, Wiley smiled. I looked to see whether it was an "eye" smile or a "mouth" smile. A mouth smile, by itself, is usually a fake. It's easy to move your lips upwards and give nothing away. A dog can do that. But an eye smile opens the soul and gives an inkling of who's inside. I looked into Wiley's eyes and saw darkness, clearly.

"Okay," Wiley said, "I'll talk to you on Wednesday. I'll be here, in Raleigh."

I released his hand, my mouth smiling, and left his house.

22.

I called a friend of mine at East Carolina to ask about Aeriel's funeral arrangements and learned that Aeriel's father and ex-minister had refused to let her be buried in the church cemetery in Asheville, causing a major rift between her parents. When the father and minister finally did agree to an Asheville burial, they learned that Aeriel had had a notarized will drawn up two months earlier, stipulating, among many other things, that she would be buried in the Welch family plot in Tarboro, North Carolina. It had been Fiona's suggestion following Aeriel's untimely outing and her father's subsequent rantings. The Welches, being a close and loving family, had of course agreed with their daughter.

Tarboro, North Carolina, is a town approximately twenty-two miles northwest of Greenville. It is an old community, dating from the early eighteenth century. One of its most notable features is a large town commons, purportedly the second-oldest in America, surrounded by houses representing the area's long and notable history. Federalist houses abut Victorian abut contemporary.

The Welch family belonged to Calvary Episcopal Church, one of

Tarboro's oldest. The church sits inside a yard and cemetery of more than three acres. The whole area is surrounded by a brick wall enclosing what could be called, if the headstones were absent, an extraordinary arboretum. Every shrub and tree imaginable flourishes in a beautiful, serene space. Paths shaded by the limbs of oak trees, maples, sweet gums, hollies, and ginkgos crisscross the cemetery in every direction.

I have been to Tarboro many times and have numerous friends from there. An unusual town for eastern North Carolina, it was an important inland port on the Tar River during the Revolution as well as a prosperous pre-Civil War community. But even more unusual is its sophistication and progressive outlook compared to that of many other small eastern North Carolina towns. Tarboro is one of the few communities where Fiona and Aeriel would have been welcomed.

Monday morning arrived cold and damp for early November. The clouds hung low, blowing over Raleigh with little promise of improvement as the day wore on. Tarboro was more of the same. I left my Raleigh hotel several hours earlier than necessary so that I could find a place to park away from the churchyard. Lucy had not asked me to attend the funeral with her and I hadn't called her to see if she wanted me to, expecting a cold response. We hadn't spoken since the afternoon she raged out of my Raleigh hotel room.

Wiley was probably right. It didn't make a lot of sense, my attending Aeriel's funeral. I didn't know her and the chance of someone seeing me and being offended was a real possibility. I just had this feeling that I should be there, even though I've never been one to trust gut reactions. I try to separate emotions from my work and to plan my emotional responses, but for some reason I couldn't do it this time, not without a nagging sense of cowardice and guilt.

Lucy didn't appreciate the complexity and subtlety required to work in the United States Senate, the necessity of separating one's emotions from one's intellect. If you start to take comments personally, you die. Who you are in a one-on-one situation changes when you go before the cameras or sit for an interview with a journalist like Lucy. One moment you're a rational human, conscious of exercising your free will, the next you're a gear in your party's power structure. Lucy didn't understand that or maybe she just didn't want to acknowledge it, but she did understand the human soul, and my seldom-used gut told me that this was a time and a place for soul-searching.

I entered the church early and secreted myself in the uppermost balcony. I wore a dark blue raincoat, a large-brimmed safari hat, and dark glasses, which, taken together on a gray day, made me look like one of the characters in the Spy vs. Spy cartoon strip from *Mad* magazine; however, looking silly was irrelevant if I achieved anonymity.

The Episcopal service was short but emotional. Five minutes into the service, a woman whom I assumed was Aeriel's mother became so hysterical that she had to be helped from the church. Since no man accompanied her, I also assumed that Aeriel's father had refused to attend.

Fiona gave a short, tearful tribute to Aeriel, followed by several emotional eulogies delivered by members of the East Carolina faculty. After a pause in the service, Ginna Humphreys walked to the front of the church and delivered an extraordinary and heartfelt salute. I can't remember everything she said, but I do remember her closing.

"Of all the tributes given today in memory of Aeriel Sopwith—teacher, inspiration, humanist, and friend, the one I believe best encapsulates her life is—artist. First and foremost she was an artist. Aeriel seemed to fly above the crass hypocrisy of our world—a world full of demagogues and Tartuffes. Through her lens she allowed us to see the beauty, truth, and joy that was *her* world. Though she was brought down in the end by those craven pretenders, she has left us the great treasure of her work and thus her soul. I shall miss her and the energy of her soul."

No names were ever mentioned, no specific events ever referred to, but it was clear that Dr. Humphreys and virtually everyone in the church that day had assigned blame for Aeriel's death. The tenets of Christianity that proclaimed forgiveness and charity towards all people would have been sorely tested had Senator Hoots or Earl Anthony been present, nor was I anxious to discover my own place in the emotions of the assembled.

Following the service, most of the congregation gathered outside in the churchyard next to and under a tent covering Aeriel's grave. Against earlier predictions, the clouds had largely dispersed and the sun was beginning to shine through the branches and remaining leaves. I had located the Welch family plot earlier that morning, thus had already scouted out an appropriate vantage point for the graveside portion of the service.

About fifty feet from the grave plot there was a small meditative space carved from the foliage. No more than fifteen or twenty feet across, a stone bench stood in the middle and large azalea bushes sheltered the back. A large tree stood next to and slightly behind the bench. There were no name plaques or head stones evident, so I assumed that it was a place provided by the church for personal reflection. I had already seated myself on the bench as the crowd gathered around the grave.

Being well away from the throng, I took my dark glasses off so I could better see the mourners. Just as the minister began to lead the assembled group in a hymn, a man tapped me on the shoulder, "Excuse me, but do you mind if I share the bench with you?"

Without looking up, I answered, "No, not at all, please do." As he sat down, I gave him a quick glance and nod of greeting. He was over six feet tall, black and wore a kind of cat-ate-the-canary smile, which seemed a bit odd. His dress was distinctly bankerish—a navy-blue cashmere overcoat over a well-tailored gray flannel suit and a pair of lace-up business shoes. He didn't say anything else, but did make an attempt to sing along with those around the grave.

Looking over the crowd, I noticed that there were very few black faces. I expected this was not a function of any bias or racial prejudice on the part of Aeriel or Fiona, simply that they hadn't had many African-American friends. With the completion of the hymn, I turned slightly on the bench, put out my hand and said, "I'm Billy Bowater."

He smiled, hesitated before taking my hand, then finally took it, looked me in the eye and said, "Christian Pope—and I know who you are." I sat there dumbfounded and for once in my life hadn't the slightest clue what to say.

Christian had no intention of ending my embarrassment, so at last I managed, "Since I don't recall ever meeting you before, how do you know who I am?"

"Do you think that administrative assistants for powerful senators are the only ones who do their homework? I knew who you were the day Senator Hooter and that phony Bible thumper from Georgia issued their kill orders on me and poor Aeriel. I've got a good friend in D.C. who works on the Hill, and I had him give me the intel on you, Carter & Holmes, and the senator. I know a lot more about you guys than you know about me. Don't you agree, Bill Walpole, Atlanta attorney and contemporary art collector."

Goddamn. How could you be so stupid, Billy. Of course, Robert Donnovon's and what was his name . . . Doc Banner. I should have seen through that. Christian, you lying son-of-a-bitch, how dare you lie better than me.

"Very impressive," I said with a smirk. "May I say that you do an excellent impersonation of an accountant, Christian, but I'm a bit disappointed that I didn't see through it."

"That's okay, what with the hat pulled down, dark glasses, jeans, and the T-shirt, I looked like the president of the Washington, D.C. Bob Marley fan club. By the way, Superman couldn't see through those shades."

Small consolation for being so clueless. I turned my attention back to the graveside, but still continued my conversation with Christian. "As far as not knowing much about you, Christian, you're right, I don't know much . . . yet. But trust me, sir, I will, and you can count on that." Christian too was looking at the grave site and speaking with only a slight turn of his head in my direction. "Don't get your shorts in a wad, Billy. I don't mean to threaten or insult you. I just wanted to show you that I'm not some hapless pawn who can be pushed into hanging myself."

"I never supposed you were, especially after the letter you wrote to my friend, Lucy Sue Tribble." Christian almost laughed aloud at this, but managed to suppress any sound for the sake of the final eulogies at the grave. Hearing the preacher's voice rise in final prayer, I indicated that we should discontinue our conversation, quiet as it was, until the service had concluded. He agreed, nodding.

Within fifteen minutes, the service now over, the congregants began to file out of the churchyard. I looked at Christian. "How come you never . . . ?"

Someone, in a voice louder than I liked, cried "Billy . . . Billy Bowater?" It was Wilson Holderness, a Tarboro-born classmate of mine at Carolina. I said to Christian, "Don't go away. I need to say hello to this guy."

I stood up, smiled and put out my hand. "Hello, Wilson, long time no see. How are you?"

Wilson shook my hand, and after telling me way more than I needed to know about his wife and kids, said, "Wish I could stay, but I gotta meet the little lady and pick up the kids. Good to see you, Billy, and don't be such a stranger." I smiled and waved at Wilson's departing back, then sat back down and looked at Christian again wearing an eye-lighted smirk.

"Too bad Wilson had to go, I was getting all excited to hear about little Wilson's appendectomy."

"Right, me too," I replied. Again I started to ask Christian why he never called to complain about all the shit we spread about him when I saw him move his gaze to someone or something over my shoulder. I turned to see Lucy Sue Tribble and Ginna Humphreys standing on the brick path not twenty feet away. I had often heard the expression "if looks could kill" but only now understood the full import. The two women stared as if they were trying to dissolve us with their eyes.

"How interesting," Lucy Sue finally said. "William Bowater the Third, scourge of the weak, and—" she took a few steps toward Christian and held out her hand, "you are?"

"Christian Pope," said Ginna Humphreys.

"Of course you are," said Lucy Sue, "Tall black man wearing a tailored suit and a cashmere overcoat. We seem to have progressed from starving artist wasting away in a garret to a rather elegant urbanite."

Christian stood up and took her hand, "And I assume that you are the exceedingly nosy Ms. Tribble who has been calling me non-stop."

"If you mean the journalist trying to write an honest account of the recent debacle that passed for a campaign, yes, I am she."

The air was growing heavy. Zingers coming in fast. I stood up, hoping to lighten the mood.

"Let me guess, you two have something on your minds other than a double date with two handsome fellows you recently met in a cemetery." Neither one cracked a smile; however, Christian seemed to have some fun with it.

Ginna, having never taken her eyes off of Christian, said, "It's good to see you too, Christian. How have you been? Oh really, well thank you. I'm glad I could help. Oh, you're welcome. No really, I'm glad that the show was able to help launch your career. You really don't need to call and write so often. I know you must be busy keeping up with galleries and museums eager to represent and exhibit you."

Christian sat back down. "Ladies, obviously you two have something on your collective minds other than, as Billy suggests, a date. Billy, may I suggest that you sit your ass down before these two knock you down." I complied, curious to see who would fire the next shot. As I expected, Lucy was the first.

Looking at me she said, "Why are you here and why didn't you tell me that you were coming?"

"I didn't tell you because I thought I might detract from what you needed to do. I didn't want to add to the emotional distress of our last meeting."

"That was thoughtful, but why did you come, my feelings aside?"

"I don't know. I just had a feeling that I should be here, that I owed Aeriel something. I went by Senator Hoots' house last Wednesday, after you left the hotel, to talk about what we should say or do concerning Aeriel's death. He wasn't very pleased at the prospect, but after a brief and very heated discussion, he decided to issue some bullshit statement expressing sympathy for the tragic death of such a young person. I haven't seen the final version, but I can imagine the sanctimonious prattle that's in it. Anyway, before I left his house, I told him I was coming to her funeral."

Lucy cocked her head to the side. "What did he say?"

"He said, as you might imagine, that that was a lousy idea and that I shouldn't come. He said that in the very near future I needed to, and this is a direct quote, 'decide where I should lie down and with whom'. As I left, he gave me a kind of mortuary smile—teeth, and soothing words but eyes that were estimating the size and cost of my casket. We shook hands, but haven't spoken since." There was a long silence. Lucy and Ginna looked at the ground as if they'd lost something. Christian was fixed on Aeriel's gavesite.

Finally Ginna looked over at Christian. "And how about you, Christian? Why are you here?" Christian didn't say anything right away. He looked at Lucy, then me and finally at Ginna.

"I'm here because I promised Aeriel that I would come."

The three of us, looking a bit shocked, waited for an explanation.

"Aeriel and I often spoke together after all the ruckus started over the Xers' show. I think I called her first, but after that she called me almost every week. Ginna, I know that she spoke with you frequently, and you should know that she got a great deal of comfort out of your conversations." He turned to Lucy, "And you as well, Ms. Tribble. She felt you were fair and sincerely cared about her."

"From me, I hoped she'd get some anger. I tried to make her mad at Hoots and Anthony; to learn to hate their hypocrisy and greed and understand that they were doing all this simply to win votes and gain crusade members, but Aeriel couldn't grasp the concept of acting in greed and hate. She saw the world as a beautiful place and figured that she must have done something to deserve such venom, that somehow she was at fault.

"I tried to tell her that she wasn't, that it had nothing to do with her. But I never won her over to understanding the dark side.

"As far as my being here, a week or so ago she said that she had a big event coming up, maybe her biggest, and that if it indeed came to pass, she wanted me to come. I told her that I was excited for her and that I also had many offers for shows of my work. We laughed over the irony that such bad reviews, such condemnation, from Wiley and Earl could work in our favor.

"In hindsight, it's obvious that she and I were talking about two different things. I have, in fact, gotten lots of new offers to show my work, while she was talking about her suicide. I understand from Fiona that she photographed her death.

"But, back to my promise and why I'm here. When she told me about her upcoming event, she begged me to come; so I told her to let me know where and when and I would be there. So, here I am."

23.

No one spoke. I looked up into the broken lines of clouds pushed across the sky by a cold northwest wind. Leaves fell over the church-yard, some gathering into small tornadic eddies that blew across the headstones and down the paths between the lines of graves. All but a few people had left the yard and those who remained were there to visit their own loved ones. Ginna, sat on the bench wiping her nose, trying to collect herself. Having given Ginna his seat, Christian now stood on the path, his arms behind his back. Following Christian's lead, I had given Lucy my place on the bench and was now leaning against the tree behind it.

Other than Ginna's weeping, the wind in the November branches was the only sound. None of us seemed to want to intrude on the others' thoughts but no one left, either. Time seemed to pass like hours but it was probably only a few minutes, Ginna wiped her eyes, gathered herself, and looked at Christian.

"So, who are you, after all?"

Christian cocked his head to the side and looked at the three of us like a lawyer choosing a jury.

"I'm Christian Pope, painter. Who do you want me to be, Ginna? "

Ginna shook her head. "I want you to be honest. I want you to be, I don't know . . . someone who feels, who is an artist for a reason. Christian, you never told us much about yourself except your address and the minimum number of clichés about art and the X generation, which, I believe, is not even your generation." Christian listened, changing his expression only slightly as she spoke.

"Ginna, why do you think you're owed anything more about me? I'm not a writer writing an autobiography. I'm not some teenage singer needing to impress an audience with my tragic life story—what I've endured and risen above. My work is all you need to know. It is, in fact, all you can know. You could never understand my history or my soul. What I see, what I feel, what I wish to say is in my work, and if I have to explain it, then I didn't do a very good job creating my art in the first place."

Ginna regarded him evenly. I, for once, understood that I had no dog in this fight, so I kept my mouth shut. Just as it seemed the door had been permanently closed, Lucy Sue stood up.

"Wait a minute! As the nosy bitch in the group, the one who wanted to tell your story to the world so it would understand what the Xers' show and its detractors were really about, I believe you do owe an explanation, Christian. You seem to be a man with some sense of loyalty and feelings or you wouldn't be here at the funeral of a dead woman you barely knew. Ginna put a lot of herself and her reputation on the line defending you and your art, so you also owe her something of yourself . . . or does that not matter to you?" Christian listened without comment but when she finished, he nodded slightly toward Lucy.

"You make a good point; however, I don't feel like reading about my life in the features section of the *News & Observer*, Ms. Tribble. I—"

"Forget it. This doesn't have anything to do with the paper. I'm here as a private citizen, not a reporter for the *N&O*. You have my word that nothing said here will ever see print." Christian looked at Lucy and then at me.

"Believable, counselor?"

I nodded. "Absolutely."

He looked at Ginna, "Okay, brief history. First, Christian Pope is my legal name. It's not the name I was born with, but then Antonius Banner, nicknamed Doc, didn't suit."

I smiled with the realization that I had, in fact, met Christian Pope . . . Pope, a.k.a. Doc Banner, before Lucy.

Christian continued, "I was raised in D.C. by my mother's sister after my mother died of an overdose. According to my aunt, I was probably ten years old when I came to her, my age being somewhat in doubt. My father was Martin Luther King Jr., or so I told myself for years. I suspect that my father's true identity would be somewhat lower on life's ladder. Aunt Maya was an exceptional woman whose taste in men was horrendous. She was largely self-educated and beautifully so. She is still alive, still lives in D.C., and still works at The Smithsonian as a housekeeper.

"Sometimes when she took me to work at night, I walked around and looked at the paintings. It was warm and quiet, and after a while I found I had developed a passion for painting. I would wander the galleries of the National Portrait Gallery for hours marveling at the images and techniques the paintings showed. When I finished high school, I went into the army, and because of my test scores, I got assigned to the signal corps. Let's say that while not illuminating from an educational standpoint, the army gave me important lessons in personal discipline and responsibility.

"After I got out, I attended American University with the assistance of a government grant and you know the rest. By the way, I'm not as old as you think I am, but I'm slightly beyond the technical cutoff for the X generation. I sort of told the truth. Anything else?"

"Why didn't you respond to any of my calls or the university's calls when we were trying to defend the show and, in particular, you and Aeriel?" Lucy asked.

"Because I wanted the shit to keep coming out. I wanted Wiley and Earl to knock themselves out screaming pervert, deviate, and queer. As I once told Aeriel, 'The only thing worse than being talked about is not being talked about.' Since the noise over the Xers' show, I've gotten at least a dozen offers of shows all over the East Coast. In fact, I'm on my way to Atlanta now to meet with a dealer who wants to represent my work."

He looked at me and with that same cat-who-ate-the-canary smile and said, "Perhaps, Bill, you could tell some of your fellow collectors at the High Museum that a Christian Pope is on the way to Atlanta." Lucy turned toward me with a quizzical expression.

"Very funny," I replied, ignoring Lucy's gaze.

Continuing his dialogue, he then looked at Lucy. "And by the way, Ms. Tribble, that terrible monstrosity of a painting, *Jordan's Water?* Robert tells me he has a client who wants to buy it at twenty thousand. Before the Xers' show, I couldn't sell the original version of that painting for five hundred. So the senator's revulsion might make me rich, or at least let me pay some long overdue bills."

Ginna's gaze moved from somewhere across the cemetery directly to Christian's face. "What do you mean, 'the original version'?"

"The basic painting, the one showing a man urinating on another man, was painted about three years ago. It was based on one of my many arresting memories from childhood. One of my early jobs was to go and find the current ne'er-do-well living with Aunt Maya and me and bring him home from whatever bar he was hanging out in. One night I found the guy, his name was Nathan something, in a bar about three blocks from home.

"He was leaning on me as we walked down the street when he suddenly stopped and looked over at some guy passed out next to a wall. Well, you know the picture. The guy owed Nathan some money and hadn't paid, so Nathan figured that pissing on the bastard would give him some satisfaction, a sort of repayment of the debt. Anyway, the image stuck with me and I kept it as worthy of a painting."

Ginna wasn't satisfied. "Why did you doctor the original for my show?"

"Your show? I thought it was our show."

"It would have been if you had ever claimed it."

Christian shook his head, "Ginna, I claimed it; I just didn't want to engage in all the nonsense that went along with it. When I learned about 'your' show from the folks at American, I was excited. I told Robert about the show and asked what he thought I should do. He said to enter some of my work but to make it edgier.

"He said that what you were looking for was exciting young painters and that my stuff was too preachy, too old. I looked at *Nathan's Payback* and decided to add a little something, something with bite. Without going into all the reasons, I decided to put a copy of the Del Verrocchio painting on the wall behind the two men. I made some modifications to his composition and gave it a new name, *Jordan's Water*.

Ginna's looked disgusted. "Well, so much for artistic integrity."

"Who said anything about integrity? You think that artists, artists of any stripe, are people of integrity? That's about as naive as saying that legislators are people of integrity. Some wise person once said the difference between a professional and an amateur writer was that a professional writes for other people and an amateur for themselves. Same goes for painters.

"I want to sell paintings. I want to make money so I can continue to do what I love. Screw noble causes and personal expressions. Let other people waste their time protesting for purity and integrity in the arts. I created *Jordan's Water* to cause a stir, to get my name out there. The fact that it caused a stir doesn't mean that it isn't a well-executed piece of art. In fact, I think it's one of the best things I've done. It also means a big pay day, the reason a professional painter paints.

"You can't name a great artist that wasn't a businessman at heart . . . Michelangelo, Da Vinci, Monet. Everyone of them had a 'workshop.' Shit, half the paintings ascribed to these men were probably painted by an assistant who was working there so they could learn enough to set up their own shop.

"Academics always want to glorify the craft as something only done by passionate, questing, troubled souls. Well, I'm troubled, troubled at being poor! And by the way, guys, I'm about as gay as ole Billy there."

I looked at Lucy. Her expression didn't change with Christian's last statement nor did it mellow. Her look said disgust, at least how she looked at me. I knew Christian's explanation of his work would not satisfy either woman, and I was tempted to say something cute like "The truth hurts, ladies," but no—not the time. When it was clear that Christian had nothing further to say, Lucy turned her gaze on me.

"So, Billy, it seems that you and Christian have a lot in common. You're both cynical realists who see the world as one big Ponzi scheme. Maybe there's a business opportunity for Pope and Bowater in the greater D.C. area? What do you think?"

I didn't want to think. I really didn't want to be part of this discussion, but obviously Lucy and Ginna were in the mood to vent. While I was not the reason, I was now the target. Christian, picking up on that, stood with his arms crossed, a wry smile creasing his face.

"Okay" I said, stepping away from the tree.

"What do I think? I think the Xers' jury was correct. *Jordan's Water* is an outstanding work of art. I think its genesis, its background story, doesn't have a damn thing to do with its value as a painting. While interesting, it's not what the picture is about.

"I think Christian is right, that it's naïve to expect those in positions of authority or influence to be of high moral character. It would be nice. It would be gratifying, but it's naïve. How many great painters have been Boy Scouts? Not Gauguin, he took dope and had a thing for little girls. Picasso was a letch of the first order. Turner died stoned. The list of troubled but great painters is long and varied, but being flawed never seemed to affect their artistic integrity, whatever that is.

"I think Christian is also right about the impossibility of knowing another's soul. We can pretend; we can wish; we can even lie, but we'll never see inside. Never!"

Lucy and Ginna, their faces blank and expressionless, looked across at Aeriel's grave. Whatever they were thinking was well hidden and beyond inspection.

"Lucy, as to your earlier question of why I'm here, like I said, I don't yet know. I know I'm not gonna recount my life's story—it's too long and of marginal relevance. You and I have for years disagreed about personal responsibility. You've questioned how I can tolerate Senator Hoots' extreme political positions versus my own. And I've told you, and will tell you again, that what Wiley says and does is his business— I'm his employee. I'm there to manage his schedule, supervise his office, and run his political machinery. I'm not there to edify his morals, and up until now he hasn't seemed to care what my morals were. Our arrangement has worked well. I've gotten a seat at the table and Wiley has maintained his muscle in Congress.

"It's the 'until now' that seems to be the problem. Until now I never told the senator he was wrong, and not only wrong but dead wrong, as in, 'Senator, you know that's not true.' Not a lot of room to negotiate there. I might as well have said, 'Senator, you're lying.' My challenge now is what to do about that. What to say once I've said too much, but that's *my* problem.

"Listening today to the life of Aeriel Sopwith recounted by her friends, I couldn't help but wonder where I fit in this tragedy. Could I have done more to stop the homophobic rhetoric? I knew it wasn't right. I told John and Wiley and Felix that it wasn't right. But could I have done more? I've told myself a hundred times that I did all I could, but then I've told myself lots of things over the years.

"So, why'd I come? I guess to sort out the bullshit from the truth. Plus, I won't have Wiley telling me who I can see and who I can't, or where I can go and where I can't."

I stopped for a moment and looked over at the two men finishing the work on Aeriel's gavesite. The flowers were being carted away, the carpets rolled up and moved. Eventually they'd replace the soil and cover it with green sod. A stone at her head would tell the world where the remains of Aeriel Sopwith lay buried, and only her photographs would tell the world who she was. I looked back at the group, focusing on Christian.

"If I understood you correctly, Christian, you don't feel that there need be a connection between character and art. That art, professional art, and commerce are very similar. They share a profit motive and, like many others, are learned professions. I find that interesting, and I think you're right. But I also think you're wrong. If you separate character, your stuff, from your work, what's your edge, your uniqueness? How do you translate your vision onto canvas without a reference point? Without an expressed personal view, how do you produce great art as opposed to great billboards?"

I looked at Lucy. She was standing in front of the bench and was clearly curious about the Bowater now speaking. Her disgust she left on the bench.

"And how do I, you might ask, give advice to Wiley, who sorely needs it, without the same stuff, the same core? What am I, then, without a core, but a cheap recitor of political clichés or a bender of laws, or a swimmer in pools of shit? Would I be anything more than a younger version of John Carter? And what are you, Lucy, if you doctor a story to make it sell, but a pawn in the money game?"

"As I was driving down here this morning, I remembered a story a friend told me. As a senior editor at *The New York Times*, he used to play a game when he interviewed world leaders. He said he imagined himself holding a long pin, a hat pin, two feet long. As the person he was interviewing spoke, he imagined pushing the pin into their body, probing for a hard core, a personal conviction so strong that the pin couldn't penetrate it. This image, he felt, gave him a sense of his interviewee's character or lack thereof.

"Somewhere around Zebulon, I stuck that imaginary pin into my own chest, and I pretended I hit an impenetrable core on the first pass. Wouldn't we all? I was in the car by myself, talking to myself, and telling myself that my core was solid.

"But like a lot of people, too often my illusions are my greatest pleasures. Sometimes I like my illusions more than I like the truth, and the truth is—I love Washington. I like playing the power game. I like the perks and the deference. I like it all. In fact, a guy in D.C. has offered me a half-million dollars a year to head up a new think tank; basically, he wants to rent my soul, and I've been thinking about it. That's a lot of money, a lot of revenue. A lot of hat pins. The question is whether renting myself out is worth it. What is my soul worth?"

I shrugged my shoulders and smiled at Lucy. I'd run out of questions, and had neither the energy nor the will to answer those I'd already asked. I closed my eyes, leaned back against my tree, and smelled the dusky odor of old leaves and dead grass. Winter's healing sleep would now gather the oaks and maples and assorted trees of the cemetery into itself until spring awoke them to a new beginning. It had been a long day out of a long year. I too was sleepy, but as a final thought I said, "On Wednesday Wiley said that I needed to decide 'where and with whom I shall lie down.' The 'with whom' part is now clear, if mutual, but the where and more importantly, the why, are still lurking on my horizon."

The wind blew a leaf-devil down the path for about ten feet, sweeping the bricks clean. Ginna looked toward the church and Christian turned up his coat collar. No one said anything more. It was clear that the collective mood had swung toward retreat. Lucy Sue was looking at me with a kinder expression than I expected—even a cautiously affectionate one. Finally, Christian took a step forward and put out his hand, "Billy, it was a pleasure. Be sure to look me up when you get back to D.C. I'm in the book under Pope, not Banner." We shook hands, and I heard myself say, "I might actually do that, Doc."

He turned to Ginna, and with a smile, opened his arms. She returned the smile, but withheld the hug.

"I don't really know what to say, Christian or Doc or Antonius, but thanks for coming. It would have meant a lot to Aeriel—and in time, I expect I'll feel the same way."

Christian nodded. "Well, thanks. Thanks for the Xers' show, for giving me a shot, for being there for Aeriel, and for teaching other Antonius Banners about art's transformative thing. And don't worry, I'm not as big a whore as you imagine. You may be proud of me someday. My aunt is." He held up a hand, turned and headed toward the high, iron gate beside the church.

Ginna shrugged and smiled. "Well, so much for that. I never imagined when I thought up the Xers' show that my life would be so upended by it." She looked at Lucy, "You ready? I need to get back to Chapel Hill."

Looking at me, Lucy said, "I think I'll hitch a ride with Mr. Bowater here."

Ginna nodded. "I'm not surprised. Thanks for coming with me, though, Lucy. You were good company on a really rough trip today."

Lucy gave Ginna a hug and said, "I enjoyed it, too, and thanks for the ride down."

"No problem. See you around, and maybe you too, Billy, if you're ever allowed back in Chapel Hill," she said with a sly grin. "There's been some talk about rolling up the streets as soon as they get word you've crossed the Durham city limits."

Lucy Sue watched her go, then turned to me. "So, Mr. Bowater, looks like you and that holly are becoming friends."

I pushed away from the tree and turned around so I could put my hand on the trunk, then looked up. "Damn, it is a holly and a big one at that."

"So, does it put you in the hugging mood?"

"With you, yes. With some prickly tree, no."

Lucy's expression changed. "I thought," she said, "based on your recent moment of introspection, that you might have reached a boundary."

"I told you I'm not into finite boundaries, that's Wiley's thing. Anyway, the holly tree marks his boundaries, not mine. If I need a boundary line and need to hug a tree to find it, I'll hug an oak.

"Oaks might be drab compared to hollies but they're stronger and live longer. I also think they're more honest. I mean, look at that massive tree over there. Unless I'm mistaken, that's a red oak. Look how upright and sturdy it is. ' Solid as an oak.' You've heard that, right? Well, there it is.

"A bit naked right now but come spring that will change. Brown will become green and life will be refreshed. Such a tree wouldn't allow its huggers to beat up on or ridicule others. Oaks, I bet, speak truthfully, but hollies, I think sometimes hollies lie.

"They show off their red berries for you, but they don't tell you that they're poisonous. Their shiny green leaves make you want to reach out and touch them, but when you do, the spines prick you. Face it, you can't trust a holly tree.

"Besides, why do I need immutable boundaries? Why would I want my life to be so rigid that there was no room for new ideas or possibilities? A strong core isn't a boundary, it's a standard, a trunk with a deep taproot. A strong core lets you walk upright and cross boundaries, especially false, uncompromising ones, and see them for what they are, tyranny."

Lucy took my hand, " Well, whatever comes of this, I think it was a good day; a sad day, but one that gave those left behind some courage." We walked out of the cemetery and into the parking lot next to the church. Lucy looked around. "Where's your car? I ain't planning on walking to Raleigh."

"I parked a block or so away, just in case the mob got violent and came after me with torches and pitchforks."

"I don't think Tarboro is like that?" she chuckled.

I shrugged and said I hoped she was right. But truthfully, you can never tell. Even a reasonable town like this one can fool you.

As I grasped the door handle, I hesitated. I looked around, and standing there, by my car, on the edge of that two-hundred-year-old commons, beside its hundred-year-old church, in a town with traditions going back beyond the founding of the country, I understood from where I had come. I hadn't been back here, back to North Carolina, for too long. Without looking at her, I said, "You know, Lucy, I don't need to be in Washington until Wednesday, if then. By way of Raleigh, for some clothes and a toothbrush, we're only a few hours from Warren. I haven't been home, at least home for home's sake, in over two years. What say we drive to Warren for a day or two? I think I need to get back home."

"You're on, William Walpole Bowater the Third. I'd love to go home with you."

Acknowledgments

This book received much-needed assistance and encouragement from both friends and family. I am particularly grateful to my wife, Jane, for her unending support, and to my friends Maya Angelou for her advice and reassurance and Stephen Fischer for his suggestions and direction. I am indebted to Linda Whitney Hobson, my editor, for her many recommendations and her professionalism in crafting this book and am especially grateful to my friend Pat Oliphant for his brilliant artistic talent in designing the cover, which gives visual interpretation to the written words.